EARLY READER REVIEWS

"This book will keep you on the edge of your seat from start to finish! Each chapter brings new challenges, which the children face with determination and mastermind ideas. I loved their quick thinking and wittiness. But what stood out most was how much they cared for and looked out for each other."

— MÉABH (AGED 11)

"I loved that there were so many mysteries mixed in with real history! One of the longest books I've read and I finished it in 4 days!"

— BROOKE (AGED 10)

"A completely brilliant storyline and great main characters. This is a top-class book!"

— ETHAN (AGED 8)

"The best book ever — I would recommend it to everyone!" "It is an ongoing adventure that will hook readers in." "We love how it is historical fiction."

— VIOLET, OSCAR AND ALL OF OLBE
YEAR 4 BOOK CLUB

"...kept me guessing with lots of exciting moments. Reading it was also a great reason for me to stay up past my bedtime! If you loved *The Secret Lake*, or *The Magic Treehouse* series, you will love this book!"

— ADALYN (AGED 8)

"*Return to the Secret Lake* is impossible to put down! I found it very very interesting! "

— REAGAN (AGED 9)

"It's exciting! I didn't want to stop reading it. I think that it's a brilliant book! "

— JULIA (AGED 9)

"Another gripping children's time travel adventure, offering fascinating glimpses into past lives and historical events. I foresee some great family discussions at the dinner table..."

— J M FORSTER, AUTHOR

"Immerses the reader in the early 1900s and is really thought provoking for middle-grade readers. A great fictional adventure and an excellent choice for connecting history with reading for pleasure."

— MICHELLE GILBERT, TEACHER

Return
to the
Secret
Lake

KAREN INGLIS

Cover illustration by Stuart Bache

Well Said Press

Published by Well Said Press 2022
83 Castelnau, London, SW13 9RT, England

Paperback ISBN:978-1-913846-07-7
ePub ISBN: 978-1-913846-06-0

Well Said Press
www.wellsaidpress.com

FOR FANS OF THE SECRET LAKE

For the thousands of readers, young and old, who have read and enjoyed *The Secret Lake*, including so many of you who have written to me asking for a sequel, or who have left reviews. This is for you — and for my new readers.

I hope you enjoy!

KEY CHARACTERS

Past Time (1912)

Gladstone Household

Sophie Gladstone
Emma Gladstone
Miss Walker – Sophie and Emma's governess
Mrs Howe – housekeeper
Eliza – maid
Henry Gladstone – father (away)
Constance Gladstone – mother (away)

Dr Abbotts – Emma's doctor
Nurse Bagshaw – night nurse

Cuthbertson Household

Lucy Cuthbertson
Lady Cuthbertson – Lucy's mother
Miss Cowley – Lucy's governess
Mrs Dunford – housekeeper
Nancy – maid
Ellis – butler
Joseph – general servant
Lord Cuthbertson – Lucy's father (away)
Arthur Cuthbertson – Lucy's brother (away)

Other

Jack
Jacob – Jack's father
Betty – Jack's mother
Sidney – Orphan/adopted brother

Recent Time (circa 2012)

Stella Hawken
Tom Hawken
Mrs Hawken – Stella and Tom's mother
Hannah – Stella's best friend
Charlie Green – ex-gardener
Mr Hawken – Stella and Tom's father (away)

A FALL

'Ouch! That's sore!' whined Emma as Mrs Howe, the housekeeper, finished dabbing the area around the cut on her shin with disinfectant.

Mrs Howe eyed the angry red patch on Emma's leg uncertainly, then carefully replaced the gauze dressing, as instructed by Doctor Abbotts the previous morning. 'There, all done, Miss Emma. You'll be fine, I'm sure. Now, get some rest. Doctor Abbotts will be back tomorrow.'

Emma let out an impatient sigh. 'This is taking *forever*,' she said in an exhausted whisper. The room shuddered, as Mrs Howe's face moved in and out of focus in the grey morning light. Emma shook her head and brushed the dark ringlets from her face, desperate to banish the tiredness. But already her eyelids were drooping. 'Such a *bore!*' she murmured, feeling herself drift off. She turned her head sideways on her crisp white pillow and was quickly asleep.

In the room next door, Sophie Gladstone, Emma's older sister, turned left then right, studying her profile in the mirror while fiddling with imaginary pearls at her chest. She'd seen Mama do it a thousand times and dreamed of the day she'd be old enough to put on rouge, and a full-length elegant dress that shimmered in the candelabra lights. Only a week had gone by since her 13th birthday, but already she was dreaming of the day she would turn 18 and attend her first debutante ball.

For their trip to the ballet next Saturday, a treat from her parents while they were away, she would wear her new peach-coloured dress.

A gentle knock at the door startled her out of her daydreams. Miss Walker, her governess, popped her head around. 'Sophie, I need a word.'

'Of course, Miss Walker. Come in. What do you think of my outfit for next Saturday? Don't you just *adore* it?' Sophie reached into her wardrobe and pulled out the dress her mother had bought for her just before leaving for Italy. 'Mama was right. This orangey peach suits me *perfectly!*' She held it up against her long blonde hair, which fell in waves to just below her shoulders.

'And look!' she added, holding up a velvet pouch.

'Mama and Papa left me this with five shillings inside, as an extra surprise to spend for my birthday!'

Miss Walker smiled and nodded, hastily rearranging the words that were about to follow. Sophie didn't take well to changes of plan, not least when those plans centred around her. But be told she must. 'The dress is beautiful, Sophie.

'Now,' she said, clearing her throat, 'about Saturday. I'm afraid there's a bit of bad news. We may have to delay. Emma isn't recovering as quickly as we had thought and even if she's up and about I'm not sure Doctor Abbotts will allow us to go gallivanting into town so soon.'

Sophie felt her chest tighten and her cheeks flush. 'But the trip's nearly a week away. *Surely*—'

'Look, I can't be sure, Sophie. I just wanted to forewarn you. I know you've been looking forward to this, but Emma's health must come first. And what with your mama and papa away I don't want to—'

'*But she's only cut her leg!* I don't know what all the fuss is about! We'll *never* get more tickets—'

'I know. I know, Sophie.' Miss Walker's voice remained calm. 'Let's see how things are tomorrow. Mrs Howe has been following Doctor's instructions, but Emma's leg isn't healing, and she seems light-headed. Now, I'll see you in the library at 11. We have Latin verbs to go through.'

Sophie clenched her teeth as Miss Walker turned to leave. The moment the door closed, she stamped her foot and flung herself on her bed. Why, oh, why, of all weeks did Emma have to choose this one to fall down the outside steps? Why couldn't she be like other girls her age and spend more time reading and learning to sew? And *why* did she and Lucy spend so much time in the gardens, anyway? She turned onto her back and stared at the ceiling rose above her, tears blurring its delicate carving. The churning in her tummy was back. She always knew that everyone found Emma smart and funny, despite — or even because of — her wild tendencies. But she had recently overheard Mama and Papa describe her as 'our *endearing* younger daughter'. When Sophie had looked that word up in her dictionary, it had given her a hollow feeling. She had never heard them talk about her like that — it seemed that she had to work so much harder than Emma to earn their affection. And now Sophie's own special day from them was about to be ruined all because of Emma.

THE RETURN OF THE MOLES

'Excellent work, Mrs Howe,' Doctor Abbotts said the following morning. 'It's still a little swollen, but she should start turning a corner soon. Carry on applying the carbolic lotion and keep the room well aired. And remember, cleanliness is vital. We don't want an infection creeping up on us. I shall see you again tomorrow.'

It had been Doctor Abbotts' third visit and his words from earlier that day swirled in Emma's head as she lay on her pillow in the early evening, looking out towards the gardens. After three days in bed, she'd had enough. Reading was impossible — even with the newly installed electric lights in her room. She couldn't keep her eyes open long enough to get to the end of a page.

Miss Walker had been kind, coming in to read,

and Sophie had come and gone, getting impatient with her as usual when she didn't have the energy to finish their game of draughts. The housekeeper, Mrs Howe, had even broken house rules and agreed to bring Harry, her beloved terrier, to see her. But right now, the person she most wanted to see was Lucy — dear Lucy — her best friend whose house backed onto the same shared gardens as her own in Notting Hill, and with whom she had shared the great adventure the previous summer. Emma and Lucy had made a pact never to tell anyone about the magical moles and the visit from Stella and Tom from the future. The only other person who knew was Jack, their odd-job man's son, and although she hadn't seen him in many months, she knew their secret was safe with him.

Most of all, Emma was intent on keeping her promise to Stella that she would try to come and see her, if *only* the moles and time tunnel would appear again. As autumn had turned to winter, she and Lucy had abandoned their weekly night-time mole hunts, and an unseasonably snowy start to the year, combined with visitors filling both houses, meant they'd only managed a few outings this year. Thankfully, April had brought warmer weather, but she was clearly out of practice sneaking out of the house after dark — falling down the steps on her way back in the other night was the last straw. Thank goodness she hadn't set Harry off barking!

It was around 3 a.m. that Emma woke. She thought she'd heard a distant dog barking, but all was silent. Her shin gently throbbed. She pulled her blankets and eiderdown to one side, reached forward and ran her fingers around the edges of the dressing. Her skin, which gleamed in the moonlight that streamed through the part-open shutter, felt hot — and smooth and tight, like polished wood. As she lay back, trying to make herself more comfortable, she heard distant barking again. Harry hadn't run off once since Stella and Tom's visit. Surely that wasn't him? She pushed the palms of her hands deep into her feather mattress and eased herself back and up to a seated position, then swung her legs over the side of the bed. She thought about turning on her bedside light, but changed her mind. As her feet found the rug, a stabbing pain shot up through her injured leg, causing her to snatch her foot up. Not daring to put weight on it again, she hobbled to the window, relying on her left leg for balance.

The dog barking had ceased, but her curiosity had not, and she folded back the tall wooden shutters to give herself a clear view of the gardens. All was still as she gazed out across the moonlit scene. She smiled, remembering Tom, Stella, Jack and herself, all huddled in a circle behind a bush, sharing secrets in the middle of the night after she'd caught them during their break-in to get food. Oh, what fun it had been! And, oh, *what* a surprise to see their shoes and boots dangling into the fireplace from the chimney flue!

She sighed gently. What were Stella and Tom doing now? Did they ever think of her and Lucy, and Jack? Would Stella be disappointed that she hadn't come to find her, as she'd promised? She hoped not. Thank goodness she had Lucy to share her story with — without her she was sure she'd have gone quite mad thinking she'd dreamed the whole thing up!

She leaned against the window for support. As she did so, the room swayed a little. Her light-headedness had returned, and her leg was suddenly throbbing more strongly. She shifted all her weight onto her good leg and reached to close the shutter. At that moment, a dog's bark echoed in the distance and as she looked out across the gardens her heart stopped. She took a quick inward breath. There, in a moonlit clearing below the trees in the middle of the lawn, a group of four moles scuttled in a circle. Moments later, they were gone.

3

LUCY'S VISIT

E mma fidgeted in her bed, trying to rearrange her leg without disturbing the dressing. She'd hardly slept after seeing the moles and was relieved finally to see morning light slipping in through the cracks of the shutters. The opening and closing of doors lower down the house told her the servants were up. Minutes later, the door opened. Mrs Howe appeared, carrying a tray with a glass of milk, a boiled egg, toast and preserves.

'Ah, awake already? How are we this morning?' Mrs Howe set down the tray on a side table.

'Much better,' Emma half lied. The truth was, her leg was still throbbing, but she wasn't going to let on. 'Can Lucy visit later? I'm *dreadfully* bored!'

Mrs Howe smiled. 'Doctor Abbotts will be here at 10. Let's see what he says.' She gently lifted the bedding and inspected Emma's dressing. 'Well, it's not perfect, but at least there's no change for the worse. There's a relief. Now, let me help you to the lavatory.'

Emma leaned on the housekeeper's arm for support as she hobbled across the room. She gritted her teeth each time her right foot met the ground as her shin sent out what felt like bolts of lightning up and down her leg.

'Are you sure you're all right, Miss Emma?'

'Perfectly,' said Emma. 'It's only a *little* sore now.' That was a lie, but there was no way she was going to risk Lucy not being invited.

'Well, the good news is you seem in better spirits today, my dear. The less good news is it's not healing *quite* as quickly as I'd like, so it's a few more days of rest for you I'm afraid, Miss Gladstone,' said Doctor Abbotts as he snapped his bag shut.

'Oh, but can my best friend Lucy come for lunch, Doctor? I'm just *dying* to see her! It's so *boring* being stuck in here!' Emma bounced an eager glance between Doctor Abbotts and Mrs Howe.

Doctor Abbotts hesitated, then smiled and nodded. 'Well, you're not infectious, so I don't see why not. Just promise me you'll keep your leg raised. Oh, and eat yourself a good lunch. Infections have a habit of sneaking up just when you think you've warded them off. Energy and rest are your allies, my dear!

'Mrs Howe, please check the dressing this evening and change it if there's any sign of weeping. I shall be back tomorrow morning. Now, I must get on. Good day, young lady, and enjoy your luncheon!'

Mrs Howe chuckled as she held the door open for him.

'Poor Emma!' exclaimed Lucy Cuthbertson, marching in through the front door. As she removed her straw hat, the early afternoon light bounced off her ginger freckles and strawberry blonde hair, which hung down her back in a thick plait, tipped with a purple ribbon. Eliza, the Gladstone family's housemaid, exchanged amused glances with Lucy's governess, Miss Cowley, who had escorted Lucy around the block from the other side of the garden square.

'Good afternoon, Miss Lucy,' said Eliza, taking Lucy's hat. 'And thank you, Miss Cowley. Please let Lady Cuthbertson know that one of us will accompany Lucy back.'

As Eliza took her coat, a door opened across the hallway and Miss Walker and Sophie appeared, each carrying books. Sophie gave Lucy a sullen stare, which didn't go unnoticed.

'How lovely to see you, Lucy,' said Miss Walker. 'Emma is so looking forward to seeing you — she really could do with cheering up.'

Sophie lifted her chin. 'Actually, I think Emma could do with *getting* up! How on *earth* can such a small cut be taking so long?'

'Sophie! We've been through this already,' said Miss Walker. 'We must follow Doctor's orders. We can't take risks, and with your mama and papa away I'm afraid—'

Sophie fixed a stare at the floor. 'I just can't believe we're missing the ballet.' The hollow feeling had returned. She knew she was being unfair, but she couldn't stop herself. She felt like a train out of control. 'And if Emma's so ill, *how* can she have visitors? Papa has *told* her about going off in the gardens before, but she never listens. Everything's ruined!' Clutching her books to her chest, she marched across the hall and into the drawing room, slamming the door behind her.

Silence filled the hallway.

'I'll go to her,' said Miss Walker gently. 'She's not been herself lately.'

'I think she's missing her mama and papa,' said Mrs Howe, who had appeared partway through the outburst.

Lucy cleared her throat. She was dying to see Emma and, if truth be told, more than a little tired of

Sophie's haughty behaviour. Why the grown-ups couldn't see she was jealous of Emma was beyond her. All the praise Emma had got after exposing their house servant Sid Crawley as a thief last summer probably hadn't helped.

'Emma!' exclaimed Lucy with a wide smile as Mrs Howe led her into the room.

'Dearest Lucy! *There* you are!'

'How *are* you? Mama told me you fell down the steps!' Lucy raised her eyebrows then slipped a sideways glance in the direction of Mrs Howe, who stood to one side but far enough back to miss the signal. 'How's your leg? Why's it up like that? How *boring* to be stuck in here all day!'

'It most certainly *is*. Beyond words! Harry got under my feet — naughty dog!' Emma curled her finger around a strand of her dark hair, her signal to let Lucy know she was 'embellishing'. 'The leg thing's to stop infection or something. Miss Walker's been reading to me, and Sophie's been in a few times to play games, but she's so *grumpy*. I can't blame her, though. We had to cancel her birthday outing.' Her eyes sparkled and she giggled. 'Oh, and I suppose I do usually beat her at Fishpond!'

Lucy sat down on the side of the bed, taking care to

keep clear of Emma's leg. 'Well, *I* am here now to save you and we are going to have a marvellous lunch, and a game of Ludo.'

Emma smiled at Mrs Howe, waiting for her to announce her departure. She was bursting to give Lucy the news.

'Now, no over-excitement, girls. Eliza will be up with your lunch presently. Remember, Miss Emma, you're to stay with your foot raised.'

'Of course, Mrs Howe.' Emma nodded vigorously and stared hard at the door, willing her away.

The moment the door closed, Emma's face lit up. 'I've seen them, Lucy! I've *seen* them!' she squealed.

Lucy furrowed her brow. Then her jaw dropped.

'THE MOLES!' they exclaimed together.

'When? Where? *HOW?* Is that why you fell? Oh my goodness! Did they trip you?' Lucy's muddled questions kept coming, stifling Emma's attempts to reply.

'Through the window — last night!' Emma finally managed.

'Oh, Emms! I can't *believe* it. After all this time!' Lucy jumped up from the side of the bed and began pacing up and down, eyebrows set high, hands splayed over her mouth. With her cream day dress and sash, and perfectly woven and ribboned plait, she looked every inch a child actress rehearsing a dramatic part. The unfolding scene sent Emma into fits of laughter,

14

interrupted only when Eliza knocked and entered with their lunch.

'As soon as I'm up, we must go on another mole hunt!' said Emma as she picked up an apple from the small fruit bowl on the tray in front of her on the bed. She'd made a point of finishing every scrap of the salmon and potatoes even though she didn't feel hungry. Mindful of Doctor Abbotts' words earlier, she knew she needed all the energy she could muster.

'Oh, I do hope they come back again! It's *such* bad timing!' Lucy paused and frowned. '—or maybe it's a *sign*? Maybe the moles *knew* you were ill and came to help!' Her green eyes widened as she bit into her own apple.

Emma almost choked on her fruit. 'Dear Lucy, you'd make a brilliant detective when you grow up, if only women were allowed!'

'Oh, but we will be one day,' Lucy declared. 'Mama says lots of things will change when women get the vote. *In fact*, I think I rather *love* the idea of solving mysteries and crimes. Imagine going to work to investigate murder! All those dead bodies and blood!'

As Emma burst into more giggles, her leg tingled and started to throb again, but she ignored it. 'Anyway, about our next mole hunt,' she said. 'I was thinking last night we should hide some clothes in that old hut on the Island for Tom and Stella, just in case they want to come back down with us. Remember how different theirs were?'

'Oh my goodness, Emms, that's such a *clever* idea! Now *you're* being the detective! I've plenty of day dresses I never wear. And there's a whole wardrobe full of Arthur's clothes now he's away at boarding school. He'd never notice if—'

A knock on the door interrupted their conversation and Miss Walker popped her head in.

'It's 3 o'clock, girls. It's time to walk you back, Lucy.'

'Already?' said Emma with a sigh. She didn't let on that her leg was throbbing more strongly. Nor that she was starting to feel tired. It was just so good to spend time with Lucy.

'Doctor's orders!' said Miss Walker with a smile. 'I'll come up and read to you later. Eliza will be up shortly to clear your luncheon away.'

'Can Lucy come tomorrow?' asked Emma.

'If Mrs Howe and Doctor are happy, I don't see why not. Are you ready, Lucy?'

'I shall see you tomorrow, Emms,' said Lucy, jumping up. She held up crossed fingers out of Miss Walker's sightline. 'And we'll make a *plan* for when you're up properly!'

* * *

It was the middle of the night, and Emma tossed and turned, trying to get comfortable. She'd woken sometime earlier drenched in sweat, and mightily relieved to escape a dream in which she was trapped inside a fire where moles danced around her in the flames.

Her clock chimed once, indicating a quarter hour. Would the moles be outside again? Moonlight seeped through the shutters, and she peered across the room, trying to pick out the gilded clock face on top of her bedroom fireplace. She pushed herself up into a sitting position to try to get a better look. The sudden change of position made her feel a little nauseous. As she put her hand up to brush her hair out of her face, her forehead felt cold and damp, which was most odd, as she was sure she'd felt on fire when she'd woken up. She didn't dare turn on her bedside light, as Mrs Howe had left her door ajar. She pushed her covers and eiderdown away and slowly swung her legs off the bed. At the moment her injured leg passed under the shaft of moonlight, she was still straining to see the time — as a result, she didn't see just how bloodied and wet the bandages had become. Her foot found the familiar rug, but as she tried to stand up her legs, jelly-like, refused to cooperate, so she manoeuvred herself around to face the bed and walked her way along using first the mattress then the brass footboard at the end for support. From here she reached for the back of a chair and hobbled towards the mantlepiece, where the clock read a quarter to three.

Still using the chair back for support, Emma hobbled to the window and pulled back the shutter. As the room lit up, it began to spin, and another wave of nausea washed over her. She forced a glance to the gardens. The moles were there again. Her mouth began widening into a smile. Then everything went dark.

4
A CHANGE OF PLAN

As luck would have it, the chair not only caught Emma's fall as she fainted, its clatter onto the wooden floorboards at the edge of the rug, taking the clothes rail at the end of the bed with it, also woke Harry, whose barks from the kitchen woke the household.

Mrs Howe, who'd taken the precaution of leaving her bedroom door open at the top of the next staircase, was there within moments, soon followed by Miss Walker and Eliza.

'Help me lift her, Eliza,' said Mrs Howe, pulling her dressing gown cord around her waist.

'I'll support her legs,' said Miss Walker, her face drawn and pale. With the lights on, the weeping wound was clear for all to see. Miss Walker exchanged worried glances with Mrs Howe as Emma started to come round.

'You're all right, Miss Emma, dear,' said Mrs Howe.

'Saw them. Again...' Emma's murmurs were hard to make out as she appeared to be drifting in and out of consciousness.

'Saw whom, dear?' asked Mrs Howe gently.

'Her forehead's burning,' said Miss Walker.

'The *moles,* silly!' murmured Emma. With eyes still shut, she gave a wide smile and shook her head.

'Get a bowl of cold water and some towels please, Eliza. Miss Walker, please call Doctor Abbotts. This fever's making her delirious. We need to keep her temperature down until he arrives.

'Now, you lie there while we clean up your leg, Miss Emma. No more moles nonsense.'

'Moles! Tell... Lucy!' Emma smiled again and sighed deeply before falling back into a deep sleep.

'What's happened?' Sophie stood in the doorway in her white ankle-length nightgown, clutching Harry, who was whining and struggling to break free.

'No need to worry,' assured Miss Walker. 'Your sister fell out of bed. I expect she got up to use the chamber pot and her leg gave way. Either that or she fainted — she seems to have a fever.' She smiled at

Sophie. 'She's muttering about moles of all things! I'm sure she'll be fine in the morning. Mrs Howe will stay with her until Doctor arrives.'

Sophie took a deep breath and rolled her eyes. 'Come on, Harry,' she murmured, just loud enough for Miss Walker to hear, 'back to your bed. At least *you* know when to stay put!' But as she walked away her cheeks felt numb, and she found herself blinking back tears. Last week, she had locked Emma out in the rain as a *sort* of joke. Could this have caused the fever? She tried to push the thought away.

* * *

'But Mama,' Lucy remonstrated, 'you said Doctor Abbotts said she's *not* infectious!' It was the second morning after Emma's night fall and the doctor had cancelled all visits.

'That doesn't matter — she has a dangerously high fever and is very confused, and her leg has swollen right up.' Lady Cuthbertson stood in front of the grand hall mirror adjusting her wide-brimmed and feather-filled hat, which perfectly counterbalanced her cream embroidered silken coat. 'Mrs Howe said the doctor's worried about *septicaemia*, which can be serious. We must let her rest, dear.'

'*Sep-ti-see-mi-a?* What's that?' said Lucy, drawing out

21

each syllable as she mimicked her mother's pronunciation. The word hissed on her tongue like a serpent.

'It's an infection that sometimes gets into the bloodstream. It can be…' Lady Cuthbertson hesitated and glanced at her daughter's reflection. 'It can make you very ill indeed. In *some* cases, it can be fatal. Now, I'm sure Emma will be fine bu—'

'Oh, Mama! You don't think Emma could *die*, do you?' The word *die* floated on a breathless whisper. Lucy's cheeks were suddenly pale, her green eyes glazed with welling tears. 'It was only a *leg cut*!'

'Oh, dear me, Lucy. Always so dramatic! No, I don't think it will come to that,' said her mother gently. 'And she certainly won't thank you for being so morose! But we must let her rest. Now, Miss Cowley is ready for you. Off to the library for your French practice, please. Then perhaps you can write a get-well note for Emma? Anything you can do to lift her spirits — Miss Cowley can take it over.'

She picked up her white gloves from the sideboard. 'I have more Suffragette meetings up in town today, but I'll eat dinner with you this evening. I think you need cheering up. Don't forget that Papa gets back from Paris tomorrow — we don't want him finding you all down in the dumps, darling.' She turned to leave. 'Oh, Miss Walker said Emma had a message for you.'

'What message?' Lucy's eyes widened.

'Something about *seeing moles again*. A lot of nonsense from the sounds of things, and she was very feverish. But at least you know she's thinking of you! I'm sure she's fine, dear.'

The front door opened and the house servant, Joseph, appeared. 'Your taxicab awaits, my lady.' He bowed his head as Lady Cuthbertson walked out of the door.

'I shall see you later, Lucy.' And her mother was gone.

Lucy found it impossible to focus during her French lesson with Miss Cowley. She normally enjoyed the tricks her governess taught her, such as 'E/ES/E' for regular 'ER' verbs in the singular. If you repeated those sequences out loud a few times, it was hard to go wrong when you came to write out a sentence. In fact, to help her remember the silent 'ES' endings in the 'tu' form, she used an extra trick by always thinking of *Emma Sister* when she wrote the word 'tu'. Emma was the closest thing she had to a sister. Her own sister, Florence, had died of a fever at age three, when Lucy was only a baby. All she knew of 'little Flo' as her mother called her, were the photographs of her posing with their older brother Arthur, dressed up for his sixth birthday.

'*E/e-s/e,*' she drilled, her voice uncharacteristically flat, as her mind wandered back to Emma and the mole message. She knew she should show more willing, and just how lucky she was to be receiving tuition in French. Her mother's determination that she should be as *prepared as any man* to work towards a profession one day had instilled in her a determination and confidence that set her apart from many of her friends — Emma being the exception. So, while Arthur, now aged 15, was away at boarding school, Lady Cuthbertson had hired a governess who was not only trained in the classics but also specialised in maths and was bilingual on account of having a French mother.

'Let's move on to possessives, shall we?' Miss Cowley's demonstrable sigh signalled her growing impatience. But Lucy didn't respond. Instead, her thoughts remained fixed on her best friend, who had lain slipping in and out of a fever on the far side of the gardens in the two days since she'd seen her. The prospect of their long-awaited mole hunt had, of course, receded. It had taken almost a year for them to reappear, and she feared they might not be around for long, but all that mattered was that Emma should get better.

Lucy glanced beyond Miss Cowley to her father's

bureau, where the photo of Arthur and Florence caught her eye. Her heart quickened as she remembered her mother first describing how Florence had gone in such a short space of time from seeming a little tired and off her food, to feverish and unable to catch her breath. The doctors had tried everything, she had said, but it was all down to *an infection that even the best remedies couldn't fight*. A week later, Flo was dead.

Lucy pushed her chair back and jumped up from the table, her mind racing. Had she been right about the moles coming to help after all? Memories and conversation snippets jostled in her head, weaving new possibilities with dangerous consequences. In that moment, she couldn't ignore them. If Emma wasn't getting better, she must make a new plan, urgently. 'I'll go!' The words slipped out involuntarily.

'Lucy?'

'Oh, I'm so sorry, Miss Cowley. I keep thinking about Emma. May we stop early? Mama suggested I write her a get-well note. Would you be kind enough to take it over? I *promise* I'll make up the time.'

5

LUCY PREPARES

With Miss Cowley dispatched to deliver her note, Lucy raced up the stairs to the second floor. The landing smelled of beeswax and turpentine, and the large round handle to Arthur's room gleamed in the morning sunlight, which streamed from her open bedroom doorway opposite. As she turned the handle, Nancy, the housemaid, appeared from the top stairs. Lucy paused and circled her finger around the smooth brass, feeling her cheeks flush.

'Missing Master Arthur, are you, Miss Lucy? He'll be home soon enough.' Nancy smiled as she hurried past, dustpan and brush in hand, before disappearing down the back stairs.

The morning light was subdued in Arthur's room, which looked west over the crescent to the houses opposite. Lucy far preferred her own bedroom, which looked east out over the gardens and so caught the early sun. If she stood on tiptoe on a winter's day when the plane trees were bare, she could just about make out Emma and Sophie's rooms on the far side of the garden square.

She made her way quickly past Arthur's brass bed, where his favourite childhood teddy bear sat alone on the eiderdown under the canopy. The mahogany wardrobe beside the window towered over her in the gloom. As she turned the key and pulled back the doors, her nose wrinkled at the smell of cedarwood, used to keep the moths at bay. Surveying the rail, she picked out a brown corduroy jacket and a pair of breeches, taking care to rearrange the hangers to hide the gaps. Arthur was short for his age, so she was hopeful his clothes wouldn't be too big for Tom, but there was *nothing to be done on that front* if they were, as Mama would say. She quickly rolled the clothes up under her arm, relocked the wardrobe, and slipped across the landing to her room, where she hid the bundle in the wooden box trunk at the foot of her bed.

Now she turned to her own 'armoire', as her mother called it, which stood beside her door opposite the window. Bathed in morning sunlight, and with its painted grey doors with floral patterns and central oval mirror, it was altogether more pleasing on the eye than Arthur's rather sombre wardrobe. Mama had ordered it especially from France last year, to 'complete' her room.

Lucy ran her eyes across the rail and pulled out a pale blue day dress. She then rummaged in her dresser and found a pair of black woollen stockings and a pale blue hair ribbon. Holding the dress up against herself in the mirror, she tried to picture Stella's face, all the time hoping they had grown at the same rate since they last all met.

Voices echoed downstairs in the hallway as Ellis, the butler, greeted Miss Cowley, back from her errand. Lucy quickly rolled up the dress and stockings and added them to the box trunk, then rushed out to get news.

'How is Emm—?' she began, from the top of the stairs. She stopped as she saw Miss Cowley in muted conversation with Ellis and Mrs Dunford, the housekeeper. Mrs Dunford shook her head slowly as Miss Cowley continued to talk in low whispers. 'What's happened? Is she any better?' Lucy descended the stairs, holding her breath.

Miss Cowley exchanged an awkward glance with the housekeeper, then nodded as Ellis took his leave. 'Come into the drawing room with us, dear.'

. . .

'You were right to be worried, I'm afraid, Lucy,' said Miss Cowley. 'This wretched infection seems to have got the better of Emma. She doesn't seem to be making any progress yet, but Doctor Abbotts says she's a fighter.'

'Will they take her to the hospital?' Warm tears began trickling down Lucy's cheeks. Only two days ago Emma had seemed her old self. *How* could things have changed so quickly? And why, oh why, hadn't she thought of her plan to find the tunnel yesterday?

'Not now,' said Miss Cowley. 'Doctor says early stage tuberculosis is rife in London hospitals, and that's when it's most infectious. The last thing Emma needs is to come into contact with it. He's brought in a night nurse and is visiting daily himself. She really is in the safest place.'

A light tap on the door interrupted their conversation and Nancy appeared. 'I wondered if Miss Lucy might need this.' She passed a white lace handkerchief, embroidered with lavender flowers in each corner, to the housekeeper.

'Thank you, Nancy.' Mrs Dunford passed the handkerchief to Lucy.

'What about her mama and papa?' Lucy said, dabbing her cheeks.

'They're trying to get hold of Mr and Mrs Gladstone, just as a precaution,' said Mrs Dunford.

'The telegram lines to Italy aren't very reliable, unfortunately.'

'One more thing, Lucy,' said Miss Cowley. 'Miss Walker feels the situation has become very stressful for Sophie, so I suggested she come to stay here for a few days if your mama agrees. With Arthur away, it might be a good distraction for you both.'

Lucy bit her bottom lip and stared at the space in front of her. Sophie had been so beastly to Emma recently, and try as she might, she found it hard to like her. But she was Emma's sister and surely this must be as shocking for her as it was for Lucy. 'Um, er... of course,' said Lucy vacantly. She just hoped Sophie was a sound sleeper. Emma's turn for the worse meant time was of the essence — Lucy would go out to look for the time tunnel tonight.

6

THE OVERNIGHT STAY

'Why, of course Sophie must stay,' said Lady Cuthbertson later that afternoon, handing her coat and gloves to Ellis. 'I trust you've had Arthur's room made up, Mrs Dunford?'

'Of course, my lady. We were just awaiting your arrival before going to collect her. I confirmed the arrangement with Miss Walker earlier.'

After the shock of Emma's news had sunk in, Lucy went back to her plan. She had no idea whether the moles would appear that night, but Emma's message felt significant, and time was now critical. If she could somehow reach Stella and Tom, they might be able to help. Surely 100 years from now there was *something* — some new type of remedy or medicine — that might help? Or a new way of doing things? She had now transferred the clothes haul into one of her spare linen laundry bags and hidden it back inside her trunk. The bag didn't feel too heavy and would fit easily in the boat. Getting out that night wouldn't be a problem. She'd lost count of how many times she'd done it before when going to meet Emma. She just hoped that Sophie slept as soundly as the rest of her household.

Sophie looked pale and drawn when she arrived, and Lucy felt genuinely sorry for her. 'You're in Arthur's room. I'll show you up,' she said, trying to brighten her tone.

'That's kind of you, Lucy,' said Miss Cowley. 'Ellis will bring up your bag in a moment, Sophie. Lucy, your mama will eat dinner with you both tonight. She'll see you in the dining room at seven. I shall see you both in the morning. I'm sure a change of scene is just what you need, Sophie.'

She smiled at them both before heading for the back stairs that led to her room at the top of the house.

'Poor Emms, I hope she gets better soon,' said Lucy as she showed Sophie into Arthur's room. A new counterpane, brighter in colour than Arthur's, adorned the bed and his teddy now sat on the fireplace mantle.

The bedside water jug had been filled, and a small electric lamp set beside it.

Sophie didn't answer. Instead, she looked around the room in silence, her lips pressed thin, her eyes expressionless between periodic, slow blinks.

'Are you all right, Sophie?' asked Lucy, more gently this time.

'I'm fine,' Sophie said abruptly, continuing to survey the room. Even as she reeled, Lucy knew this was a lie. Sophie's expression seemed to hover somewhere between boredom, disdain and fear — Lucy just couldn't decide which.

Lady Cuthbertson entered the dining room wearing a full-length silk embroidered dress and her hair piled high on her head. 'I've just spoken to Mrs Howe on the telephone. She assures me they're doing everything they can for Emma. Her temperature's still very high, I'm afraid, but it's stable at least. It's just a case of getting it to come down.' As she seated herself at the head of the table between Lucy and Sophie, her teardrop earrings shimmered under the chandelier light.

'Is she awake?' Lucy asked, eager for something beyond temperature updates.

'Mostly sleeping,' replied her mother. 'That's not a

bad thing, though. Doctor Abbotts says it means she's fighting the infection.

'Now, how are *you*, Sophie, dearest?' she said, turning to her. 'This must be very stressful without your mama and papa here. You know, you may stay as long as necessary until Emma is back on her feet.'

Lucy darted a glance at Sophie, ready to gauge her expression. She had invited her into her room once she'd unpacked, but Sophie had said she needed to lie down before dinner. As a result, they'd barely exchanged words since her arrival.

'I'm all right, thank you, Lady Cuthbertson. Just a little tired, really. Harry's been *impossible*, waking the household up. I'm sure once Emma's better and Mama and Papa are back from Italy everything will get back to normal.' She breathed in deeply and forced a smile just long enough to convince her hostess — but not Lucy — that all was well.

'Well, you can catch up on your sleep here,' said Lady Cuthbertson. 'And I'm sure Lucy is delighted to have the extra company, what with Arthur away and Emma out of sorts.' She smiled as she picked up her soup spoon. 'You may start, girls.'

Delighted to have the extra company couldn't have been further from the truth as far as Lucy was concerned. Yes, she felt sorry for Sophie, but on the other hand her aloofness despite Lucy's best efforts to engage with her was rude and unnecessary, especially with poor Emms so ill. Worse, her presence in the house was an added complication for Lucy's plan — what if she woke in the night and discovered Lucy gone? After all, it was Sophie who'd come and shouted the house down when she, Tom and Stella had come that night to rescue Jack from the cellar. The look of triumph on Sophie's face in that moment had remained etched on Lucy's mind for weeks afterwards and came back to haunt her now. Each time Lucy bowed her head to scoop up more soup, she stole a furtive glance up at Sophie, trying to read her emotions. But her brown eyes rarely strayed from the pink rosebuds that decorated the edge of her soup bowl, and the few inches of white tablecloth beyond it. For now, she was giving nothing away. Emma had been right about Lucy's detective's instincts, Lucy realised — she loved trying to solve puzzles.

'How was your meeting today, Mama?' she asked, suddenly desperate to take her mind off the Sophie complication and her impending plan.

Lady Cuthbertson led the conversation for the rest of the meal, vividly describing the Suffragette meetings she'd been attending at Caxton Hall, how two members of their group had forced their way into the Houses of Parliament to disrupt a debate, and how *marvellous* it was to be joining forces with women from so many backgrounds. At that point Sophie had briefly widened her eyes and cleared her throat. This went unnoticed by Lady Cuthbertson, who was in full flow, but was not lost on Lucy, who suspected Sophie would have a hard time mixing with anyone below her class, never mind the cause. She was so *stuffy*, and always seemed so cross — the complete opposite of Emma, who'd have made best friends with the scullery maid's daughter given half the chance.

'We're doing this for you, girls!' Lady Cuthbertson finally remarked. 'And for *all* the women who work in this house.' She picked up the bell beside her and rang it. Ellis, the butler, and Mrs Dunford entered to clear away the dishes. 'Please thank cook for the especially delicious mutton, Mrs Dunford.'

Sophie put her hand to her mouth to hide a yawn.

'No desserts for us tonight. I think we're all a little exhausted,' said Lady Cuthbertson with a quick smile at Sophie and raising herself from her chair. 'I think early nights all round are in order.'

It was just after 10 o'clock that Lucy heard voices in the hallway below. She'd been in bed for two hours and, as far as the household was concerned, was now fast asleep. She crept from her bed and opened the door a few inches, straining to hear.

'Should we wake Miss Sophie, my lady?' The concern in Mrs Dunford's voice was clear.

'No, there's no point worrying her. Doctor Abbotts said things could still change. He's promised to call again if it turns critical and we can arrange to take her over. Let's all keep our fingers firmly crossed for better news in the morning. Now, let's try to get some sleep.'

7
THE MOLE HUNT

The house had been silent for an hour, during which Lucy had been tossing and turning as her mother's words *'if it turns critical'* replayed in her mind. Blinking back tears, she tried to push away thoughts of what that might mean.

The hallway clock chimed midnight, and on the final stroke she made up her mind — for Emma's sake she must stop worrying and *focus on her plan*.

She and Emma normally met by the lake at 1 a.m. She would stick to the same routine, to be sure that everyone was asleep. Rowing across wouldn't be a problem, as she and Emma usually took it in turns, though pulling the boat in might be trickier. She would place the bag of clothes at her feet in the centre of the boat. With a full moon, the light would be good.

The more she thought about it, the more she

thought it would make sense to hide the bag of clothes somewhere near the shed, rather than inside, just in case anyone came looking. There were a few old gardening tools in there, including a rusty old hoe, which she could use to dig a hole out of sight.

Visualising each step in this way was a welcome distraction and calmed her nerves. However, her eyelids were starting to feel heavy and were soon fluttering.

The clock chimed 1 a.m. — startling her awake. She sat bolt upright, her breathing fast and shallow. *How could she have been so careless to have fallen asleep?* She pushed off her eiderdown and lowered her feet to the ground, taking care to sidestep the creaking floorboard beside her bed. Shaking, as she tried to control her breathing, she slipped off her nightdress and pulled on her undergarments, a simple purple day dress and black stockings, then took a coat from her armoire. As she opened the box trunk at the end of her bed, it gave out a loud squeak. She froze, holding the lid half open as she strained to listen for signs of life in the house. Silence. Letting out a shuddering breath, she opened it a little farther, retrieved the laundry bag, then gently lowered the lid back down. This time, it remained silent.

Next, as she had done so many times before, she

took one of her pillows and a cushion and pushed them under her eiderdown to give the impression of a child asleep below the covers. She then tiptoed towards the door, placed the laundry bag on the rug, and got down on her hands and knees. With her right cheek squashed against the floorboard, she closed her left eye and squinted through her right under her doorway to the room opposite. No sign of life, or of light.

Lucy was well practised at stealing out of her room in the middle of the night and was soon silently descending the stairs, heading for the door to the back stairs and lower floor. Her garden boots, as they all called them, sat in a small cloakroom beside the kitchen back door. Just as she reached the hallway, a distant thud interrupted the silence. Her cheeks flushed hot, and she froze. She remained still for a good minute, straining for the sounds of footsteps. The rope ties of the laundry bag began cutting into her fingers under the weight of the clothes, but she resisted the temptation to change her stance, for fear of creaking a floorboard or jinxing herself in some other way. But only the gentle ticking of the hallway clock broke the silence. It must have been her mother or Sophie turning in their bed and knocking against the wall. At last, she slipped through the entrance to the lower floor.

As always, she had left her black leather boots laced so that she had just enough room to squeeze them on and off without needing to undo or redo the laces all the way down. She and Emma had worked this out between them, knowing that every second might count if someone woke on the nights they went out. Even after one of the servants cleaned them, Lucy would sneak back down and adjust the laces to the required spot. This nocturnal stealing around required careful planning, and Lucy normally thrived on the challenge, not to mention the spine-tingling excitement and danger of it all. Tonight, however, was different. A hollowness in the pit of her stomach had replaced her usual sense of anticipation, along with the fear that if she were caught, the one hope of finding a cure for Emma would be dashed. What's more, she would have no way of explaining herself away. Time was critical, and Emma's life depended on her. She *must* reach Stella and Tom, whatever the cost.

A light breeze brushed her cheeks and hair as she stepped outside. She closed the kitchen door and looped the drawstring ties of the laundry bag over her right shoulder, then tiptoed up the steps. The bushes around her swayed in the moonlight, casting eerie dancing shadows across the small courtyard garden in front of her. She glanced around, then darted forward and passed out through the low wrought-iron gate into the communal garden beyond. Once out of sight of the house, she breathed a sigh of relief.

The moon cast dappled silver patches across the lawns in between the clusters of oak and plane trees whose leaves rustled below the star-filled sky. Checking the coast was clear, as she always did when on her way to meet Emma, Lucy headed in the direction of the lake. Where the moles might appear, she had no idea. Emma had first seen them from her room in a clearing between the plane trees; Stella had seen them by the lake when they'd first arrived down the time tunnel; Tom had seen them in the distance, back in their own time where there was no lake. And on the night of Sid Crawley's arrest in the gardens, Jack had seen them by a cluster of bushes not far from where they had all gathered.

The more Lucy thought about it, the more she was convinced that *where* the moles appeared was less significant than *when* they appeared. She had said this half-jokingly the other day to Emma, but maybe it made sense? After all, they had appeared for Stella and Tom when Jack was in trouble, hadn't they? And now they had appeared when Emma was in trouble. She was certain that Emma's garbled message about the moles wasn't feverish dreams at work. She must have seen them again that night after she saw her, and Lucy now strongly suspected the moles had come for one reason — to help her find a cure for Emma. The weight of responsibility felt heavy and frightening, but it also made her even more determined to see this through.

Within a few minutes, she reached the narrow path between the rhododendron bushes that led the 20 yards to the lake. The trees were denser here, blotting out the moonlight. Unperturbed, she marched on, the bag on her shoulder brushing against the bushes on either side in the dark. About halfway towards the lake, a rhododendron bush she had just passed rustled violently. Lucy stopped and turned. It was too dark to make out much more than the outlines of the bushes, which continued to sway either side of the path.

'Who's there?' she demanded in a low voice. Oddly, she felt less afraid than irritated that she might be about to be found out. The bushes and trees only swayed and rustled in response. It must have been a bird in the undergrowth, or her bag disturbing a branch. She turned and carried on walking.

As the path bent gently left, the lake came into view, its surface lit up by the moon. She breathed out, relieved to be leaving the darkness behind. At that moment, a dry twig snapped behind her.

'Who is it?' she demanded again, spinning round.

The bush closest to her rustled.

'It's me!' Sophie stepped onto the path, wearing an

overcoat over her long white nightdress, and ankle-length boots. She pushed a blonde ringlet away from her cheek, then jerked her chin forward and glared at Lucy. Her eyes, which caught the moonlight filtering down between the trees, reflected a strange mixture of anger and fear. 'Exactly *what* are you doing out here?' She darted a look at the bag. 'And *what* is in that bag?'

Lucy's lips hovered apart as she stood staring at Sophie. She was normally quick to improvise in sticky situations, but her best friend's older sister always left her struggling to string more than two words into a coherent sentence. And even when she managed it, like earlier this evening when Sophie had arrived, she had just felt plain stupid — as if she were making conversation *for the sake of it* in order to please Sophie Gladstone. *Why* did some people have that effect on you?

'*Well?*' demanded Sophie. She folded her arms.

'I…' Lucy turned to point towards the lake, hoping that in the few seconds this afforded her she could conjure up a story. Her heart skipped a beat — there in the distance, on the far side of the water, a group of four moles scuttled in a circle at the foot of a tree.

She spun back towards Sophie, anger and courage coursing through her veins. 'I'm going to get help for

Emma,' she said in a low and firm voice. She put her hands on her hips. 'Don't you dare spoil this, Sophie!' Her cheeks flushed warm as the words tumbled out. The bushes swayed and the leaves rustled loudly, as if in support.

'By *sneaking* into the *garden* at nigh—?'

'*Listen!*' Lucy fixed her eyes on Sophie's. 'You almost messed things up for poor Jack last year. Please don't put Emma's life in danger. Now, follow me and do as I say!' She pressed her lips together and furrowed her brow as she turned and started marching towards the lake. The moles continued their dance for a few seconds more before vanishing.

Where she had found the courage to take on Sophie, Lucy couldn't say. Whether it was from her own inner strength or somehow from the moles, it didn't matter. It felt right, and it felt good. If Sophie tried to shout the house awake now, she was prepared — but in that moment something told her this wouldn't happen.

'Where are you *going*?' whispered Sophie crossly, following behind. 'And how *dare* you speak to me like that!' Her tone was remonstrating, but at least she wasn't yelling for help.

The path ended, and they found themselves on the bank of the lake. The boat was tethered in its usual place against the jetty. 'I can't explain,' said Lucy, marching to the boat and untying it. 'Here, take this while I get in.' She thrust the laundry bag into Sophie's arms. 'Now, do you want to come with me or wait here? I don't know how long it's going to take, but there's not much time.'

'I, I...'

'What?' Lucy waited for her reply, but Sophie simply stared beyond her at the water. 'What *is* it?' Lucy let out an impatient sigh. How strange their roles seemed to have reversed in such a short space of time.

Sophie cast her eyes down to her brown laced boots, then rolled her eyes and sighed in return. 'I... I'm scared of the water. I'm not a strong swimmer.'

'*Oh.*' Lucy gave her a blank stare, hastily gathering her thoughts. Emma was like a duck in water. It had never occurred to her that Sophie wouldn't be too.

Lucy glanced to the far side of the lake. If Sophie stayed behind and went back to the house now, she might get caught and spill the beans on her. And even if she didn't get caught, Lucy couldn't be sure she could trust her.

'You'll be fine. It's not far, and it's not that deep,' said Lucy. She crossed her fingers behind her back. In fact, she had no idea of how deep the lake was, but she hoped that *in these extenuating circumstances*, as her mother would say, this little white lie would help persuade Sophie to join her. What the next step of the plan was, she didn't know. She'd have to make that bit up as they rowed across.

Sophie passed the bag to Lucy, who sat in the centre of the boat with her back to the pointed bow. Lucy leaned forward and stowed the bag under her seat, which consisted of a horizontal wooden plank. Sophie crouched down on the jetty and reached for Lucy's helping hand. 'Sit down at that end in the middle as soon as you're on,' said Lucy.

As the boat wobbled under Sophie's weight, she let out a low whine, like a kitten.

'It's fine. Trust me.' Lucy smiled and fixed her eyes on Sophie's as she crouched onto the seat at the back end. 'Stay in the middle like that and stay facing me. You can tell me when we're getting close to the bank.'

The gentle splash of the oars on the lake brought a welcome calm after what had felt like a prolonged altercation but, in fact, had been only a few exchanges of harsh words. As she rowed, Lucy felt Sophie's eyes boring into her. Meanwhile, in an attempt to gather her thoughts and avoid more questions, Lucy fixed her own concentrated stare on the moonlit water and turned her head periodically to check their direction.

'I heard what Mrs Dunford said,' Sophie blurted out, her voice cracking. 'Do you think Emma might die?' The raw fear with which she delivered her question so took Lucy aback that she briefly lost her grip on her left oar, causing the boat to veer to the right and wobble violently. *'Help!'* Sophie shrieked, as Lucy quickly corrected their path.

'Sorry. It's all right. We're nearly at the other side,' said Lucy quickly. 'I'm going to turn the boat to the right. Grab onto the bank as soon as you can and try to pull us in. I'll row the other way to help.' She felt ashamed for ignoring Sophie's question about Emma, but feared she might burst into tears. Besides, she needed to take one step at a time and was still formulating her story.

The 'landing' went more smoothly than Lucy had dared hope and she was soon on the bank tying the boat to an old tree stump near the edge of the water. Sophie passed out the laundry bag, as instructed, then cautiously raised herself from the boat and scrambled out while Lucy gripped the sides, trying to help keep it steady.

'Well?' said Sophie. Safe on dry land, she had changed her tone.

'Follow me. There's something I need to do, then I'll explain. I promise.' Lucy blinked hard, trying to stay focussed, as she continued to ignore Sophie's questions. She turned and headed for the path that led to the disused gardener's shed. The Island had been better maintained in earlier years, and she and Emma had often poked their noses inside the shed, wondering if it might have a connection with the time tunnel. But all they'd seen were a few rusty gardening implements strung together by cobwebs, including the hoe which Lucy would use to scrape out a hole. She halted as a sudden fear struck her. If the household woke and came looking and found the boat, they'd probably think they'd drowned!

'*What?*' whispered Sophie from behind.

Lucy closed her eyes. *Focus on the plan, the rest will follow,* she told herself. Her mother *might* have said something like this once, but she wasn't quite sure. 'It's fine,' Lucy whispered back. 'Just a bird.' And she marched on towards the shed.

Finding a soft spot of earth to bury the laundry bag was easier than Lucy had expected. Even more convenient, it was hidden behind a group of small bushes that backed onto the shed, making it harder to spot. Sophie paced up and down, hands on her hips, as Lucy scraped away a hole, lowered in the bag and covered it with earth. Not once did Sophie offer to help. Tears of frustration clouded Lucy's eyes. Her back was aching, and time was short. Worst of all, she was now stuck with Sophie and had no idea of how she would even *begin* to explain her plan. She smoothed over the last of the earth and looked up — into a dark silence. Sophie had disappeared.

'Well, if you're going to hide it, you'd better do it properly.' Sophie was standing behind her, holding two broken branches with a few twigs and leaves still attached, and a couple of large stones. She stepped forward and threw them haphazardly over the area, marking the hole Lucy had just dug. 'That'll do!'

Lucy stared at Sophie. 'Thank you,' she said, trying to keep her voice firm. She lowered her chin and studied her boots. 'Look, I'm sorry about everything. Follow me and I promise I'll try to explain.'

Soon they were back at the tree where the moles had danced, and which she and Emma knew from their conversations with Stella, Tom and Jack in the garden a year ago, was the one that led to the time tunnel. 'We'd better sit down.' Lucy hesitated as she glanced into Sophie's eyes, which remained stern and mistrusting. 'What I'm about to tell you is going to sound completely mad and unbelievable, but you're going to have to trust me — I think Emma's life might depend on it. And you must *promise* not to interrupt me until I finish—'

'All right, all right. Just *tell* me!' Sophie's voice was shaking as she lowered herself to sit beside Lucy.

'Well,' said Lucy. She brushed an imaginary hair

from her cheek. 'You know my cousins, Stella and Tom, who came to visit last year? You know — when poor Jack was accused of stealing?'

'Of course.' Sophie's voice was suddenly small and a little distant. It was she who had ruined their plan to help Jack escape that night by shouting the house down. She had never apologised to Emma or Lucy since, which hadn't surprised Lucy.

Lucy paused as she stared out at the lake where the boat rocked gently in the night breeze. She then switched her glance to Sophie. *Say it as it is,* she told herself. 'Well, they're not my cousins at all.'

Sophie shot her a puzzled frown.

'And I know this is going to sound utterly mad,' she went on, 'but they're actually from another time *in the future* and I think they can help Em—'

'*Pardon?*' Sophie's angry glare had returned. 'What *on earth* are you talking about?'

Lucy felt the blood drain from her cheeks.

'From the *future?*' said Sophie, scrambling to her feet. 'Did you really think I'd fall for that? I can't *believe* you persuaded me to get in that boat!'

Waves of nausea washed over Lucy. How stupid to think Sophie would believe her! *Why* hadn't she just made up some silly story about sleep walking and led her back to the house?

Just as Sophie reached her feet, a movement on the

far side of the lake beyond her caught Lucy's eye. She jumped up beside Sophie and peered across. There were the moles again, scurrying in a circle — though much faster than before.

'What are you looking at?' demanded Sophie, following Lucy's gaze.

'*Quick*, we have to go! The moles! Time's running out!'

'*Moles?* Go wher—'

'Up here!' Lucy glanced up into the tree canopy above them. 'Follow me!' She reached for the lowest branch. 'Or you can stay here if you want. But I don't know how long I'll be gone.'

Sophie stamped her foot. 'I've had enough of this, Lucy Cuthbertson. I was a fool to follow you in the first place. I should have woken your mama—'

'Oh, *please* hush up! Just follow me — otherwise, I'll see you later.' Lucy then grabbed the lowest hanging branch and hoisted herself up.

8

THE TIME TUNNEL UP

As Lucy started climbing, the branches around and below her trembled, then began to shake. She glanced down to where she could just make out Sophie. She'd made it to the first branch. This was a good sign, though Lucy sighed inwardly, wondering how she would cope when they entered the time tunnel, not to mention when they emerged into the future. If only Sophie had let her finish her story.

'*Wait*, will you!' Sophie's voice was cross and breathless.

'You'll have to keep up!' Lucy called back.

'I can't believe this! Can't we just go back to the house? *Stupid* lake, *stupid* boat...' Sophie's voice was cracking.

'Keep climbing. Trust me!'

Lucy continued to move up through the branches,

feeling her way in the dark. She and Emma had practised climbing the tree many times since Stella and Tom's visit — including with eyes closed — so she knew the route to the top. Of course, they had never found the time tunnel, but, then again, they had never seen the moles since last year's adventure. The tunnel would be there this time, of that she was sure.

The trembling of the tree trunk and branches, and the occasional frustrated *Ouch!* told her that Sophie was still with her. 'Keep going!' she called.

With her left hand gripping a small stump — one of several she had just encountered but didn't remember from their daytime climbs — Lucy reached up with her right hand to find the next one, when the tip of her fingers struck something metal. She snatched her hand back and sucked her nails to ease the searing pain. *'This must be it,'* she whispered.

She splayed out her fingers and reached up again, slowly feeling her way in the dark. As soon as she located the ladder rung, she folded her fingers around it in a firm grip. Now, standing on tiptoes on the branch below, she let go of the small stump that she'd been clinging to with her left hand, and reached up and felt around in the dark moist air above her. Very quickly, she came up against what felt like earth — the earthen wall that Tom and Stella had described so vividly.

Reaching up a little farther, she located the second ladder rung.

'I've found the time tunnel!' she called out, in that moment realising this would mean nothing to Sophie. But there was nothing to be done.

Lucy gripped the second ladder rung and pulled herself up off the lower branch and stepped onto one of the short stumps she'd been holding on to previously. As her head entered the mouth of the tunnel, a shroud of darkness enveloped her, banishing the slivers of moonlight she'd been relying on to help find her way. Her eyes darted up and down, left and right, searching for a way through the wall of black. Her breathing was short and hurried in the moist, cloying air. She twisted her face to her left. As she did so, her nose brushed against the earthen wall. She jerked her head back in surprise, striking the wall of the tunnel behind her. Her whole body was suddenly trembling, and she found herself loosening her grip on the upper rung. She paused and took in a shuddering breath as she stared up into the darkness. Tears began welling. She couldn't do this.

'Where *are you*? I should *never* have trusted you!' Sophie's voice echoed in the distance, jerking her out of her trance. Lucy glanced down, her lower leg dangling mid-air, ready to take her out of the tunnel.

'I'm here! Keep climbing.' she called back feebly, all the time realising she couldn't carry on herself.

'*Lucy! Answer me!*' Sophie's voice was both angry and pleading, and seemed even more distant than before, even though she should surely be closer by now.

Lucy looked up one last time, high into the tunnel, ready to start climbing down. As she did so, the light seemed to adjust, as if someone had pulled a veil away. Or perhaps it was her eyes becoming accustomed to the dark? Either way, the wall of black softened into a deep grey, allowing her to make out the sides of the tunnel and the shadowy outlines of the ladder running up the side.

It's now or never! It's now or never! The words came from nowhere, echoing in her mind. Had they come from the tunnel? There was something about them, as though from a memory, that urged her not to give up.

'Follow me, Sophie!' she called down one final time, but already she knew Sophie couldn't hear her. And already she knew Sophie wouldn't find the tunnel. She swallowed hard, blinking back the tears. *'I'm so sorry, Sophie,'* she whispered, then reached up to the next ladder rung.

. . .

The climb up, though daunting at first, quickly became more manageable as Lucy worked up a rhythm of step and grasp, pacing her breath in time with each reach for the next ladder rung. As well as keeping her moving, focusing on this rhythm distracted her from becoming overwhelmed. The damp walls of the tunnel pressed in on her in the gloom, like a dark tower threatening to collapse over her. Actively observing her surroundings — as she was now doing — helped her stay calm in the confined space. However, when a pool of light from above appeared, she let out a deep breath, realising just how close she had come to giving in to panic. Her need to get out was now urgent, and she began climbing more quickly, her breath shorter and out of rhythm with her steps. Finally, she emerged on all fours from the last ladder rung to the inside of a bush, where sunlight seeped in from all sides, creating dappled lacework on the earth and fallen leaves.

She sat back on her heels and peered out towards the gardens, relief flooding through her as she breathed in the clear air. Then a lump rose in her throat as she pictured Sophie, abandoned and alone in the dark on the Island below, and Emma in her bed, her life in the balance with the fever. The weight of responsibility to fix this was now hers alone. *'Please let this work,'* she whispered to herself.

9

AN UNEXPECTED GUEST

S tella sat hunched over her desk by the window, finishing the last French exercise. It was 5 o'clock on an unseasonably warm Good Friday afternoon and she'd decided to get the last of her holiday homework out of the way. 'Done!' she whispered triumphantly. She raised her right hand to eye height, holding her pen between her thumb and forefinger and, after a moment's pause, let it fall to her desk. She then closed her exercise book, jumped up, and flung herself onto her bed. Stella always did the pen dropping thing when her homework was complete. Where it had come from she couldn't remember, but her mum often said that she wished Tom would get more practice at it.

She grabbed her phone from her bedside table. *Homework finished! CUL8R!* Her texting speed never failed to impress her friends. Georgina's pinged thumbs up text message came back almost instantly. Hannah's followed a few seconds later. It was Georgina's 13th birthday 'Make-up and Pizza' party later. She couldn't wait — parties these days usually meant last-minute 'sleepovers', as in a lot of chatting and not much sleep!

She lay back on her bed, smiling. Their move from Hong Kong to London last summer had worked out brilliantly. She loved her school and had made friends quickly. Even better, her best friend Hannah's family had moved back at the start of the year too and were now also living in London, not far away in Kensington, and Hannah had joined her school.

As the months had gone by, Stella had slowly pushed her and Tom's time tunnel adventure to the back of her mind. After the initial shock of Mrs Moon's death, she had quickly found a quiet peace, made easier by the old lady's promise that they would all meet again when Stella and Tom were much older.

For Tom, however, it had been harder. He was desperate for the moles to reappear so that he could go back and meet up with Jack, and during the first few weeks after Mrs Moon's funeral he had insisted they go out looking for them most days at dawn. However, as summer turned to a wet and windy autumn and school started, Tom made new friends, and his requests became less frequent. Finally, picking her moment on one particularly cold and wet morning in late October,

Stella announced that if the moles were going to come back, they would do so whether or not they went looking for them. 'Besides,' she had reminded him, 'Mrs Moon seemed to say we'd all meet much further in the future, didn't she? So what's the point of looking for the moles now?'

To her relief, Tom had slowly nodded and said, *Yeah, I guess so.*

Tom was about to be nine, and this was the first sign that the new older Tom *would* sometimes take 'no' for an answer. On the one hand, this was good. On the other, she secretly knew she'd probably miss the more stubborn Tom one day.

Why last year's adventure had pricked her mind in this instant, Stella had no idea. It happened rarely these days and tended to be of her own choosing when she was alone for a day and had time to reflect properly. Still, the moment passed, and she jumped up from her bed and flung open her wardrobe. She still hadn't decided what to wear for Georgina's birthday.

She was just reaching for one of her party tops when a loud crack, like a whiplash, echoed around her room, making her jump. She spun round. Her bedroom door was closed, so it couldn't have come from the landing. One of the French doors to her little balcony was open, so it might have been the wind knocking something over, but nothing on her desk or chest of drawers had fallen over and she couldn't see anything on the floor. Besides, there was no wind.

She returned to her wardrobe and was just re-reaching for the top when the crack echoed again. She closed her wardrobe door and went out onto her little balcony, which looked over the gardens. The neighbours' children from next door had been playing out there with friends earlier, but they were nowhere to be seen. She frowned and shook her head, then turned to go back inside, then yelped as her bare right foot landed on something sharp and jagged. She snatched her foot up, balancing on her other leg to inspect the damage. Three small stones matching the gravel from their patio garden clung to the sole of her foot. She brushed them away and rubbed at the crevice-like impressions they had left before placing her foot back down. She then retrieved the stones, along with several more she found, and threw them back out to the patio.

As she turned to go back inside, the branches of a rhododendron bush about 20 metres into the gardens shook violently. This was a favourite hiding place for next door's children and one from which they often based their 'hide and seek' headquarters. She smiled to herself. 'I KNOW YOU'RE IN THERE!' she called, half playfully and half in her mother's grown-up voice.

Then she added, in a singing voice, so as not to scare them too much: 'IF YOU BREAK MY WINDOW, YOU'LL HAVE TO PAY FOR IT!'

'Everything okay up there?' Stella's mum appeared in the patio garden, clutching a bunch of keys.

'Yeah — just some little kids throwing gravel at my window. I've told them they'll have to pay for it if they break it!'

'Always works!' said her mum, laughing. 'I'm going to get Tom now. Back in half an hour. Dad should be landing in New York any time. If he calls the house, tell him I'm in the car so I can't pick up my mobile — I'll try him when I'm back.'

'Sure thing!' Stella twirled a blonde lock around her finger. 'Oh, Mum? Can Hannah stay over tonight after the party?'

'Of course, dear — as long as it's okay with Elspeth. Just be sure to tell her we have a sitter tonight. I'm at Anna's play, remember.'

Stella gave a puzzled frown. 'Why would Elspeth even care?'

'She won't. But it's good manners to let her know. See you later!' Her mother blew her a kiss and disappeared back into the house.

As the front door slammed, Stella was already texting Hannah. *Mum says you can stay but to tell your mum we have a sitter. She says she won't mind so no idea why I have to tell you???!!!*

Lucy crouched back inside the rhododendron bush, her breathing light and jittery. Finding the house and seeing Stella from a distance was the first step in her plan. Now that she knew it was the right room, she would come back after dark when no one was around. The danger of sneaking over, not to mention seeing the puzzled faces of the young children she had encountered, had made her skin tingle. But suddenly the enormity of her lone mission overwhelmed her. She felt tearful and exhausted. Realising she hadn't slept that night, she gently let herself down on all fours and lay down on her side to rest and think. Her coat provided a perfect blanket, and the fallen leaves on which she rested her cheek felt soft and warm on the spongy earth. *One step at a time,* Mama always said. This was certainly the first important step towards helping Emma. But what lay ahead? Tiredness washed over her, and her eyelids were drooping. She pulled her stockinged knees up to her chin. *Nothing that a good sleep won't sort out.* Yet more of Mama's words. She willed herself to stay awake, in case someone found her there, but soon she drifted off.

· · ·

When Lucy started awake, she found herself lying flat on her back. She didn't know how long she'd slept but looking up through the branches she could see a night sky. Oddly, it seemed to be bathed in yellow light, which didn't look like moonlight. She turned over and manoeuvred onto all fours, trying to avoid the branches and twigs that brushed against her hair, then crawled to the edge of the bush. As she parted the branches, she gasped. All around the communal garden, the windows of the houses were lit up with square and rectangular blocks of light — many from top to bottom. Of course, she knew this was electric light, but there was *so much* of it. Tom and Stella had talked about all the things it was used for and couldn't believe it when she and Emma had explained it was quite new in their time. Not all the houses in *their* garden square had electricity yet, but even where they did, as in her and Emma's houses, thick curtains or shutters blotted it out at night, and it certainly wasn't this crisp and white. And none of the houses she knew had electricity at the top of the house where the servants slept. Just *how much* light did people need? She blew gently through her lips and puffed her cheeks out as she stared all around, realising just how unprepared she had been for the changes she would find.

Her stomach rumbled loudly. She crawled backwards into the bush and found a comfortable place to sit, then took out the apple and cheese she'd brought along from the kitchen. As she nibbled alternately on each, she realised she'd need to wait until all the lights in the square — or most of them at least — went out before trying Stella's window again. She couldn't risk being caught now, not after what she'd been through.

* * *

It was 9.45 p.m. when the stretch limousine organised by Georgina's parents dropped Stella and Hannah back to Stella's house.

'Hey! *You're* supposed to be in bed!' said Stella, lowering her eyebrows into a fake frown at Tom as she and Hannah walked through the door.

Sandra, her favourite babysitter, appeared. 'He was just going! *Weren't you*, Tom!' She winked at them all.

'Yeah! I was on my way up when you rang the bell. Ha! Ha!' He crossed his eyes at Stella and Hannah. 'What's going on with your faces, anyway? You look *weird.*'

'*Ummm*, it's called *make-up!*' Stella crossed her eyes in reply, then giggled. 'Oh! Sandra, this is Hannah. Hannah — Sandra. She's the *best* sitter!'

'Hi Sandra. Hey, Tom!'

'Nice to meet you, Hannah. I hope you girls had a good evening — you're looking very glamorous, I must say.' Sandra stood back and nodded approvingly as she looked them up and down with a smile. 'And I love your braids, Hannah!'

'The make-up lesson was *so* cool! What do you think of my eyeshadow?' Stella glanced at her reflection in the hall mirror, batting her eyelids slowly. 'The lady running it said coral and champagne go with blue eyes and pale skin.'

'What about mine!' said Hannah, joining her at her side. She flicked back her long dark braids, then peered right up against the mirror, blinking slowly. 'It's called tea-rose. She had an *a-m-a-z-i-n-g* selection for brown skin.' Her gentle Scottish accent stretched the word out like elastic.

Tom faked a loud snoring noise.

'Okay, everyone up,' Sandra said. 'Your mum's back in an hour and I need you all in bed or she might not let me come again!'

'Mum said we can watch a movie on her laptop,' Stella whispered to Hannah.

'Hey, can I watch too?' Tom spun round as they mounted the stairs.

'Nope! Girls' sleepover! Girls' film,' said Stella. 'Besides, you've just watched the whole of *The Matrix* and you're only nine.'

Tom halted with his back to them in front of Stella's bedroom door. '*Night,* Tom!' said Stella firmly, and she gently pushed him forward, giggling. As he glanced back with a cheeky grin, she blew her little brother a kiss, then piled into her room with Hannah.

'Night, all!' Sandra called up after them. 'Don't forget to brush your teeth. You too, Tom. Oh, and take your make-up off, girls! Sweet dreams, and I'll see you next week.'

* * *

Lucy crawled out from the bush and stood up, a shiver running through her from the cold. It felt good to stretch her legs after so long sitting and crouching. Her black woollen stockings felt a little damp as she dusted off the old leaves and clumps of earth that had stuck to them.

Only a few lights remained on in the square — well away from Stella and Tom's house. As a result, the gardens were now bathed in familiar moonlight, providing a comforting reminder of home. She crossed her arms and put her hands in her armpits, to help keep warm. Staying close to the bushes, she edged her way towards Stella and Tom's house, her eyes fixed on Stella's window.

As she approached their courtyard garden gate on tiptoe, her black lace-up boots sank into the soft grass, making a gentle squidging sound, just as happened so many times on her mole hunts with Emma. Tears pricked at her eyes as she pictured Emma lying ill back at home. She shook her head. *Focus,* she whispered. She pushed open the wrought iron gate, then bent down and grabbed a handful of gravel stones.

It was hard to judge distances by moonlight, and her first few aims fell short of the balcony. Instead, the little stones ricocheted off the front of the building and rained down into the lower ground floor well, which, in her time, led to the kitchen. A piercing *miaow* cut through the silence and a black cat darted up from the well and shot past her to the gardens beyond. She froze, her heart beating heavily. Nothing stirred.

She stepped back a few paces to get a better sightline and transferred more stones from her left hand to her right. She reached up and aimed. This time they reached the balcony, but not the window.

'Fiddlesticks!' she whispered. She bent down to gather up yet more stones and took aim once more. CRACK — a group of three or four stones struck the window. She ducked down behind a small rose bush that was growing out of a large pot and peered up. Nothing. She waited a minute more, then crept out and took aim one more time. CRACK — the stones hit the window again. This time she stood up, legs apart and hands on hips, staring up at the window in her dark coat, willing Stella to appear. Still there was no sign of life. She sighed in frustration. Now what? She dropped her arms to her side — just as a small white light appeared and seemed to be moving around in Stella's room. She put her hand to her chest and half crouched down, keeping the window in view but ready to duck out of sight if she needed to.

While Lucy was outside, Stella was dreaming that she and Hannah were at a make-up party where the Queen of Hearts from Alice in Wonderland was showing them how to put on foundation, lipstick and eyeshadow in front of a huge, gilded mirror. Stella was exchanging worried glances with Hannah, who kept shaking her head and secretly pointing towards the Queen's face make-up that was so thick it looked like cement. As the Queen became more insistent, now pressing orange cream onto Stella's face, she tried to shout 'Stop!' but nothing came out. It was at this moment that Tom had appeared, reflected in the mirror at the back of the room with a large whip, which he started cracking over a stone table, as if trying to draw the Queen away. Stella smiled at Hannah in the mirror, thinking just how clever and brave and loyal her little brother was for coming to their rescue. It was the second crack of his whip that startled her awake.

'What was that?' whispered Stella, sitting bolt up.

She reached for her phone and flicked on the torch, cupping the light under her hand. Hannah, out for the count on the zed bed across the room — and snoring loudly, as usual — mumbled '*Yes!*' then turned over to face the wall and resumed her snoring.

Stella smiled as she swung her legs round and jumped out of bed. The noise had come from the window — just like earlier. She tiptoed across and opened a couple of slats of her new wooden shutter. The gardens were bathed in moonlight, but she couldn't see any movement. Then a wild thought struck her. *Could Emma have returned?* Taking care to prevent the shutter knocking and waking Hannah, she folded the right side back fully, then raised her torch and held it against the window. If anyone was out there, they'd see her. As she continued to gaze out towards the gardens, a movement directly below caught the corner of her eye. She switched her glance into the patio below just as the silhouette of a young girl in a dark coat, ankle-length boots and ringleted hair stepped into view.

Stella's hand flew to her mouth. '*Oh, wow!*' she breathed. '*Oh, **wow!**'*

Stella looked round in panic at Hannah, who, still snoring, remained facing the wall. Of course, she'd told her best friend the whole story after Hannah had eventually moved back from Hong Kong. And even though she had sat there, open-mouthed, nodding and asking all the right questions in her soft Scottish accent — about the children's clothes, what their home looked like inside, and what governesses and olden day policemen wore — Stella wasn't sure her best friend had believed her. Certainly, when Stella had mentioned the moles, Hannah's eyes had seemed to glaze over, and she'd reached for a magazine. She probably thought Stella had invented the whole adventure to help her cope after her family's sudden move back to the UK before her. Either way, Stella knew she was far too loyal to confess to doubting her and, in many ways, leaving things as they were suited them both.

Luckily, the clunk of the key turning in Stella's balcony door was drowned out by Hannah's snores, which rebounded off the wall. Stella pushed the door handle down, eased the door open and slipped out, gently closing it behind her.

As she looked out again to the patio, her heart stopped. The girl was nowhere to be seen. Stella leaned over her balcony, scanning left and right and out towards the gardens. Surely, she couldn't have imagined this. Or had she? *'Emma!'* she called in a whisper. *'Is that you?'* She stared at the spot where she could have sworn the girl stood just moments before. Then, just as her balcony door creaked back open behind her in the breeze, the girl stepped from behind the rosebush. Stella's eyes jumped wide. *'Emma!'* she called in a whisper.

'No. It's me, Lucy!' came the whispered reply. *'Emma needs your help!'*

Stella felt the jab of the door in her back.

'What's going on, Stell?' Hannah pushed out onto the balcony beside her and put on her glasses. *'Eeek!'* she breathed in her soft Scottish accent. 'Who's that girl?'

Stella glanced from Lucy to Hannah and back again, her pale blue eyes shining in the moonlight. 'It's Lucy, from the time tunnel!' she said in a high whisper. *'Quick, we have to let her in. I think Emma's in trouble.'*

She leaned out over the balcony. *'Wait there! I'm coming to get you!'*

'Is this for real?' said Hannah, taking off her glasses and rubbing her eyes, as Stella closed the balcony door behind them. 'I'm dreaming, right?'

Stella clutched her best friend by the shoulders. 'No. It's for *real*, Han! It always was real! You'll see. Wait here.' She grabbed her dressing gown from the back of the door and slipped out.

· · ·

Stella unlocked the kitchen door that led to the patio garden and stuck her head out.

'*Down here, Lucy. Down the steps,*' she called in a whisper. She held up her phone light to guide the way. Lucy appeared at the top of the steps and raised her hand to her eyes to blot out the glare. '*Oops, sorry!*' Stella re-angled the torch to light up the steps.

As Lucy descended, and as Stella took in her elaborate coat and ankle-length boots, a rush of memories from last summer's adventure washed over her. 'Oh my goodness! I can't believe you're here!' She reached out and gave Lucy a tight hug, then stepped back into the doorway. 'What's happened? Is Emma okay?'

As Stella's words tumbled out, she knew they needed to get upstairs. 'Quick — we need to get your boots off. I'll help.' Staring at the intricate laces, she realised they may be there for a while.

'No need,' said Lucy, and bent down and whipped each boot off. '*Mole hunt practice!*' she murmured with a quick smile, then shook her hair off her face and gathered her boots up under her arm.

'Follow me!' whispered Stella, pressing her forefinger to her lips. She gently closed and relocked the kitchen door and led Lucy up the stairs with the light of her phone torch cupped behind her palm.

NIGHT PLOTTING

Hannah had switched on Stella's side lamp and was sitting waiting on her bed in her nightshirt. Her glasses magnified her large brown eyes, which, as Stella and Lucy entered the room, fixed on Lucy's billowing coat sleeves, black-stockinged legs, and the muddied laced boots she clutched in one hand. Hannah hesitated for only the briefest of moments as she took everything in. 'Here,' she said softly, jumping up. 'Let me take those for you. I'm Hannah.' She smiled at Lucy, then darted a look at Stella before reaching for the boots. In that split second, Stella knew that whatever Hannah may have silently thought before, she now believed everything. Stella breathed an inward sigh of relief.

'How lovely to meet you, Hannah,' said Lucy. 'Thank you so much. They're rather muddy, I'm afraid.' Her eyes darted wildly around the room as she clearly tried to compute her surroundings. 'Oh, dear me. I'm *roasting*,' she suddenly said, starting to unbutton her coat. 'I'm so terribly sorry for surprising you like this, Stella.' She slipped the coat off to reveal a pale purple dress with long sleeves and frilled cuffs, and a panel of lace around the neckline.

'*Wow!* That's so pretty!' said Hannah.

'Oh. It's just an old day dress,' said Lucy with a quick smile, pushing her strawberry blonde ringlets behind her shoulders. 'Emms and I always wear them on our mole hunts. They're much more practical than our smart dresses. Besides, Mama would have a *fit* if she found me climbing trees in anything new!' Hannah looked on, eyes wide, lips slightly parted. 'Oh, but *poor* dear Emms!' Lucy went on. She raised both hands and pressed her fingers against the edge of her eyes, which were suddenly moist with tears. '*That's* why I'm here, Stella.'

'What's happened?' Stella felt her stomach turn as she reached to take Lucy's coat.

'She's terribly sickly with a fever. Doctor Abbotts can't control it and I'm really afraid she might die. Just like my sister Flo—'

'Why don't you come and sit down on the bed?' said Hannah, taking her hand. 'There's room for us all on here. Come on, Stell.'

A lump rose in Stella's throat as she tried to take in what Lucy was saying. She quickly put Lucy's coat on the zed bed, then joined the others. Thank goodness Hannah was here. Her best friend had a natural instinct for comforting anyone in trouble, which always had a calming effect. Stella often told her she should be a doctor or nurse when she grew up, although Hannah insisted she wanted to be a singer, *in musicals preferably*.

'Has she got flu?' Stella positioned herself the other side of Lucy from Hannah. All three girls sat with their backs to the wall, their legs flopping off the side of the bed.

Lucy gave a puzzled frown — then her eyes, still wet with tears, widened. 'Oh, *influenza*. Oh, no. It's definitely *not* that. Not consumption either. It's not *catching* or anything. No, she fell down the outside steps.' She paused, glancing left then right. 'Well, what I *mean* is, she fell down the steps outside *her* house — you know, like the ones I just came down, except they look different, of course.' She sat forward and hugged her knees to her chin. 'It was after she'd been with me on a mole hunt — she got a big cut in her leg, which didn't heal.' Her voice wavered. 'And… And then she got a fever, and now it won't go away, and Doctor Abbotts said it might be *critical*.' She dipped her chin to her knees and burst into tears.

76

Hannah and Stella each put their arms around Lucy's shoulders.

'Don't worry, Lucy,' said Hannah gently. 'I'm sure we can help *somehow.*' She glanced helplessly at Stella behind Lucy's back and mouthed, *'Now what?'*

Stella bit her lip and shook her head, then her eyes rested on her mother's laptop, which lay closed on her desk. 'Hey, let's search online,' she whispered.

'Genius!' breathed Hannah.

A breeze outside rattled the French doors and the girls momentarily froze. 'It's just the wind,' whispered Stella, letting out a breath. She leapt off the bed and opened the laptop.

Lucy looked up. 'What's *that?'* she gasped, wiping her eyes with her dress sleeve, as the white glare reflected off Stella's face.

'A laptop!' said Hannah with a giggle.

'What's a *laptop?'* Lucy's voice was high and curious as she emphasised the 'p' in the middle and again at the end, as if trying out the word for sound.

'Um, it's a kind of... er... computer,' said Hannah.

Lucy frowned as she let her legs drop down and off the side of the bed. 'Oh dear, I haven't the faintest idea what that is, but it looks *jolly,* um, interesting...'

'Oh, wow!' whispered Hannah, realising Lucy wouldn't know anything about computers in her time.

'It's got lots of information in it,' said Stella. She

scanned the screen as her fingertips tapped furiously at the keyboard. 'And there's this place called Google where you can ask questions and get answers. Look! I've just typed in *Flu* and all these results come up telling me what it is and how to cure it.'

Lucy stood beside Stella staring down at the screen and the endless entries all relating to Flu. '*Oh, my!* Are those *photographs* in there? I can't believe this!' she said, pointing at the screen. 'Just wait until I tell Emms!'

'*Yep.* See, this is a photo of the flu virus,' said Stella. She zoomed in to read the paragraph under the image. '*Flu comes from a virus and is catching. The symptoms are similar to those for fevers that are not catching and are caused by other events such as an infection.*

'Right,' she said, 'so let's try *fever not catching.*'

'Or how about *fever after a cut?*' said Hannah.

'Ooh yes. That's better!' Stella tapped the keys and hit the search button. A page of results filled the screen.

'Where's it all coming from?' gasped Lucy.

'Electricity!' volunteered Hannah.

Stella twisted round and gave her a goofy frown. 'Err... I don't think so exactly, Han!' Then she smiled. 'Electricity makes it work though!'

'So where *does* it come from?' Lucy's green eyes shone in the glare from the screen.

'Not sure. But it works through the Cloud,' said Stella, twisting back to the screen. Her cheeks flushed as she realised she hadn't the faintest idea of how the Cloud worked or how all this information ended up in her bedroom on the screen in front of her.

Lucy's mouth fell open. *'The clouds?'* she whispered.

'Cloud,' corrected Hannah in her soft Scottish accent, with a sideways glance and a smile that suggested she fully understood how it all worked after all. 'It's not an *actual* cloud though,' she added, frowning at the screen.

All three girls were now bent over, scanning down the results.

'What's that word, Stell? *Septi… Septica…'* Hannah pointed at different entries on the screen.

Lucy snatched her hand to her mouth. **'Septi-see-mia,'** she said, her voice breaking. 'That's how you say it. Mama told—'

'Sepsis and fever,' whispered Stella, focusing on a shorter headline. 'This must be it.' She clicked the mouse and highlighted a block of text in yellow, causing Lucy to step back as tears filled her eyes.

Keeping her voice low, Stella read out the definition: *'Septi…'* She hesitated. *'Septi-ca-e-mia, or sepsis, is the clinical name for blood poisoning by bacteria. It is the body's most extreme response to an infection. Sepsis that progresses to septic shock has a…'* She paused and blinked at the screen. *'…has a death rate as high as 50 percent, depending on the type of organism involved. Sepsis is a medical emergency and needs urgent medical treatment. Symptoms: Fever.'*

Lucy covered her face with her hands. 'It must be it. Mama said Doctor Abbotts said something about *preventing septicaemia.'*

Stella read on: *'Wounds, sores, or burns make sepsis more likely. When your skin is torn, bacteria on the outside can get inside. Most of the time, you're not going to get sepsis when you have a cut or wound.*

'Look! It might not be.' She tried to sound hopeful as she pointed at the last sentence.

Hannah put her arm around Lucy. 'Don't worry, Lucy. We're going to help. Quick, Stell, what does it say about a cure?'

Stella typed *Sepsis treatment or cure* into the search bar. The page filled with more results. She scanned down. 'Okay. It's talking about antibiotics.' She read out again. *'Antibiotic treatment for sepsis varies broadly with what is infected, how at risk you are for certain types of bacteria, resistance…* blah blah…' She scrolled down further and read out again. *'If you have mild sepsis, you may receive a prescription for antibiotics to take at home. But if your condition progresses to severe sepsis, you will receive antibiotics intra….* er… *in-tra-venously in the hospital. This method helps the medicine get into your bloodstream quicker so it can fight the infection sooner…'*

'That's when they put a tube into your arm,' said

Hannah with another smile and sideways glance. 'You know, like on *Casualty*.'

Stella opened a small notebook which lay on her desk and wrote down some of the antibiotics listed in the article. 'Wow, these names!' she said.

'What's *antibiotics*?' asked Lucy.

Stella was already typing into the search bar.

'It's a type of medicine,' Hannah replied.

Stella stopped and stared at the screen. 'Oh — except antibiotics aren't invented in Lucy's time. That explains it.' The search results for 'Antibiotics history' had flashed up. All three girls read in silence. *In 1928, at St. Mary's Hospital, London, Alexander Fleming discovered penicillin. This discovery led to the introduction of antibiotics that greatly reduced the number of deaths from infection.*

Hannah bit her lip and fiddled with one of her braids as she glanced sideways at Lucy.

Something behind them creaked. Stella's hand flew to her chest. She glanced back as another gentle gust of wind rattled the French door.

'You know what that means, don't you?' said Stella, turning back to the screen. 'We need to get some antibiotics to take back.'

'*Antibiotics?* Take back where?'

All three heads swivelled. Tom stood in the doorway in his pyjamas, bleary-eyed and frowning.

'What's going on, Stell?' And as his eyes met Lucy's, they jumped wide.

Tom felt his chest rising and falling as he glanced from Stella to Lucy and back again, listening to Stella's explanation. They all now sat back on the bed, and as he breathed slowly in and out, cheeks slack, he kept pinching the skin above his left wrist, fully expecting to wake up.

'I'm sorry it's such a shock, Tom,' said Lucy. 'Poor, dear Emms.' She pushed her back against the wall beside the bed and drew her stockinged knees to her chin once more.

'I hope we can help. I'm sure we can,' he whispered. Then he pressed his lips together. He was desperate to ask whether she had news of Jack, but with all minds focused on Emma and antibiotics, that would have to wait.

'So,' said Stella. 'It looks like we need to find a way to get the antibiotics.' She opened her notebook. 'Here are some it said might work for skin infections.' She held them up for everyone to see: *Flucloxacillin; Cefadroxil; Tetracycline; Cefalexin.*

Tom was frowning. 'Don't you need a doctor to get medicine?'

'My uncle's a doctor!' said Hannah brightly.

'In *Edinburgh!*' said Stella. She grimaced at her best friend.

'Yeah,' said Hannah, 'but my cousin Jade's studying medicine in London. They're all going to be doctors. Maybe she can help?'

'We need someone we know we can trust not to tell on us,' said Stella. She sighed and tapped her chin with the corner of her notebook. 'It's *so* complicated!'

Hannah let out a large yawn. 'I'll text Jade when we wake up, just in case.' She glanced at Stella's bedside clock. 'Eeek! It's 3 a.m. Shouldn't we agree a story for the morning?'

'Good point!' said Stella.

'The *morning?*' Lucy's eyes widened in alarm.

'Of course!' said Stella with a gentle smile. 'We can't get medicine in the middle of the night!'

'But your mama and papa—'

'Don't worry. I'll just tell Mum you're new at school and we invited you back — she's pretty cool about things like that. Dad's away anyway.' She grinned broadly.

Hannah frowned. 'Except wouldn't Sandra have told her if you'd had another person to stay?'

'*Maybe* or maybe not. That last sleepover we had, Mum had no idea there were four of us here 'til the next morning, remember? Sandra just assumed it was arranged.' Stella yawned and put her hand to her mouth. 'Besides, Mum won't be seeing Sandra 'til next week, and she's hardly going to bother calling her about finding an *extra* guest!' Stella turned to Tom. 'If she says anything, just pretend you knew Lucy was here.' Phrased this way, it somehow didn't feel like asking him to lie.

'Sure thing,' he whispered, nodding solemnly.

'Okay, you'd better go back, Tom,' Stella whispered.

Tom nodded and opened his mouth into a yawn. 'Night, everyone!'

Stella jumped up and pulled open her chest of drawers. 'Here, Lucy, you can borrow these PJs and we'll go top and tail, and I'll lend you some clothes in the morning. We always swap things at sleepovers!'

Hannah held the wardrobe door open while Lucy changed out of her dress and into Stella's pyjamas, out of sight of them all.

'Here — have my pillow. I don't need it,' said Hannah, taking the one on her zed bed and placing it at the tail end of Stella's bed.

'Thank you so much,' said Lucy. Stella lifted the duvet as Lucy crawled in, then lay back, clearly exhausted.

Hannah climbed into her zed bed where she pulled a corner of her duvet in to create a makeshift pillow.

'Night, Stell. Night, Lucy. I'm zonked!' she called in a whisper.

'Me too!' Stella whispered back, easing into her bed and taking care to slide her legs away from where Lucy already lay gently snoring. 'We'll just have to work something out tomorrow.' Then she switched off her light.

11

TOM'S BRAINWAVE

'Morning, girls! Did you have a good make-up party?' Stella's mum marched across the room and pulled back the shutters. 'You know it's 10 o'clock! What time were you all up to last night?'

Stella groaned and turned over, then opened her eyes. For a split second, her mind blanked as she watched Hannah stirring. Then, just as Lucy's warm leg brushed up against her under the duvet, she remembered. She took a quick inward breath and sat up to see Lucy rubbing her eyes and staring all around the room.

'Hello, there, I'm Stella's mum, Rachel. I don't think we've met, have we?' Stella's mum, dressed in sports shorts and a fluorescent orange running top, held a mug of steaming coffee in one hand as she beamed at Lucy.

'Um, this is—' Stella started.

'Hello, I'm Lucy,' said Lucy. 'I've just joined Stella's class. She kindly invited me back.' She grinned broadly, then kneeled up and held out her hand. 'How nice to meet you.'

Stella felt her cheeks burning as her mother paused, smiling, before reaching to shake Lucy's hand. 'Well, it's jolly nice to meet you too, Lucy. And what lovely manners, I must say!'

'Stella kindly lent me her *Pee-Jays*!' said Lucy. Stella felt herself blush again, but Lucy's overemphasis simply drew another broad grin from her mum.

'Well, with all the friends she has to stay, it's just lucky we have a drawer *full* of PJs!'

The wardrobe door clunked behind them. As they looked round, Hannah popped her head from around the open door. 'Just getting dressed!' she said brightly. Stella glanced in panic at the chair by Hannah's bed — then let out a slow breath. Lucy's coat, dress, and boots had vanished.

'Okay, girls, there's cereal and bread downstairs. Help yourselves. I'm off for my run. You can tell me all about last night later. Tom's only just up too. Heaven knows what he got up to last night — it was like trying to wake the dead just now!' All three girls exchanged glances as Mrs Hawken turned to go.

· · ·

'Whoa!' said Hannah the moment the front door slammed. 'You were awesome, Lucy!'

'Agree!' Stella held up two hands with ten fingers fanned out.

'I only *introduced* myself,' said Lucy with a puzzled look.

'I mean the stuff about Stella's class!' said Hannah, rummaging in a rucksack and pulling out a pair of jeans and a T-shirt. 'That was *genius!*' She started pulling on her jeans, hopping on one leg. 'And your mum's always so laid back, Stell!'

'Yeah. But she *can* be annoying sometimes.' Stella giggled and scrambled off the bed as Hannah battled with her long braids, which covered her face as she pulled her top on.

'Phew! Finally! What do you think of my new T-shirt?' Hannah twirled on the spot.

'Are those *girls* on there?' Lucy crawled forward on the bed.

'Yep! They're called Pixie Mix,' said Hannah with a wide smile. 'They're *so* cool.'

Lucy wrinkled her nose. 'How on *earth* do they get on there?'

'Um, printing, I think.' Hannah glanced sideways uncertainly.

Stella was at her chest of drawers, hurriedly pulling out garments. 'Right, Lucy, I'll lend you some clothes.

Try these.' She placed a small pile onto the bed next to Lucy, whose mouth widened into ever larger circles as she held each item up in turn: a long-sleeved white T-shirt, a pair of flowery leggings and a pale blue track suit top.

'It's all seems so *thin!*' she said, eyes wide.

'I'll hold the wardrobe door for you if you want to get changed,' said Hannah.

Lucy glanced at Stella, who was pulling on underwear and leggings under her nightdress. 'I'll be fine here, thank you,' she said quickly. She pulled off her pyjama bottoms to reveal white embroidered cotton knickers that reached halfway down her thigh and ended with a lace trim, threaded with pale pink ribbon.

'OMG! They're *amazing!*' said Hannah.

Stella giggled. 'Um, I don't think they'll work with the leggings.' She opened another drawer and pulled out a pair of white knickers. 'Here, borrow these. They'll be less bulky.' She grinned, seeing Lucy's alarmed face. 'Don't worry, they're clean!'

Lucy reddened. 'Thank you. Actually, I *might* get changed over there after all,' she said shyly. Moments later, she stood in front of the mirror. 'How *mad!*' she declared. 'If Mama could see me now!' Her face dropped. '*Oh*, and dear Emms...'

'Don't worry. We're going to make a plan,' said Hannah gently.

'Here. Try these sandals,' said Stella. Lucy slipped her feet into the flat red strapped sandals while Stella bent to tighten the buckles at the back. 'They're a bit big, but they look okay—'

Three quick knocks on the door, followed by two more, interrupted the conversation.

'That's Tom's *code knock*,' said Stella, standing up and pulling a goofy smile. 'Well, *except* in the middle of the night when he decides to sneak around!' She glanced towards her eyebrows. 'You may enter!' she called.

Tom entered, dressed and ready for whatever the day brought them.

Ten minutes later, after they had shown Lucy the bathroom and all giggled as she marvelled at the modern plumbing, they sat around the kitchen table. Lucy feasted her eyes on the colourful boxes of cereal and juice cartons left out by Stella's mum. It was only now she realised just how hungry she was. She poured herself some *muesli*, following Stella's lead, but as she tried to eat, a growing hollowness in her tummy took hold. She lowered the spoon she had just put to her mouth. 'I wonder how Emma is?' she said, her voice trembling. 'Oh, *dear*. And what about *Sophie*?' The scene before her blurred into a kaleidoscope of shapes and colours.

'It's going to be okay,' said Stella, moving beside her and putting her hand on her arm. 'The time hardly changes when you're away. Only an hour or two had passed when Tom and I came back, even after we stayed overnight in the garden.'

'Really?' Lucy glanced at Tom.

'*Yep!*' he said, and gave her a wide grin.

She let out a deep breath. 'Oh, thank *goodness!*'

'Exactly! Now eat some more,' said Stella. 'You must be starving!'

'You're right! *Full tummy, sharp mind*, as Mama says!' Lucy smiled around the table, then picked up her spoon.

At that moment, Hannah's phone bleeped. 'Cousin Jade!' she announced. She tapped on her phone and paused, then read out the message.

Hi Hannah. How lovely to hear from you! Wow, that sounds like an unusual school project! The short answer is that the only person who can write a prescription is the doctor after they see the patient. And the only person who can collect it from the chemist is the patient, or someone who knows them well and has permission to collect for them — eg a parent or carer. And, of course, you should never give someone else's medicine to a different person. I hope that helps! Let me know how the project goes! Lots of love, Jade xxx

The children's faces all dropped. Stella felt in her back pocket for her notebook where she'd listed the antibiotics that could help with early sepsis. 'Now what?' she breathed. Their mission suddenly felt hopeless.

Tom's spoon clattered into his bowl. 'I think I've just had a brainwave!' he declared.

The door slammed and Mrs Hawken appeared through the doorway.

'Good breakfast, all?' She smiled and winked at Lucy as she dropped her keys on the side. 'Great taste in clothes, Lucy — just like Stella, eh!'

'Ha! Ha!' Stella raised her eyebrows and smiled at Lucy.

Mrs Hawken pulled up a chair and poured herself a glass of orange juice 'Now, how was last night's party?'

12

THE SEARCH

After helping clear the table and *stack the dishwasher* — a term which led to puzzled looks from Lucy and hurried whispers from the children — they finally headed out into the garden.

Lucy had played along about the party and late-night movie, though got a little carried away describing the *'white face powder and rouge just like Mama's'* that they'd all had applied at the make-up session. At this point Stella and Hannah had exchanged alarmed glances and Hannah had leapt to the rescue.

'Your Victorian accent is *so* funny!' she'd said with a smile, stretching out the word *so* in her gentle Scottish way. 'You should audition for the school play!'

'Actually, it's an *Edwardian* accent,' Lucy had replied, flashing a mischievous smile at Hannah and Stella, and making Stella choke on her orange juice.

Now that Lucy knew time was more or less standing still in the past, she felt it meant Emma couldn't get any worse, for now at least. With this immediate worry off her mind, she felt more at ease.

'Goodness,' said Mrs Hawken, 'I didn't know it was a *vintage* make-up party — how novel!'

'Aye, it was,' Hannah said in a soft whisper. She then glanced sideways, trying to remember what *vintage* meant.

Stella, meanwhile, fixed her stare on the tabletop and clenched her teeth as she tried to keep a straight face.

'So what's the brainwave idea, Tom?' said Stella as they passed through the patio garden gate.

'Wait 'til we're out there,' he murmured. 'Have you got your phone?'

'Of course. Come on. Quick, everyone!'

They reached the Island and sat down on the mound. *'So?'* said Stella.

'Right. I know this might sound bonkers,' said Tom. 'But what if Charlie Green could help?'

'Who's he?' said Hannah and Lucy together.

Stella and Tom exchanged brief glances, during which Stella narrowed her eyes just enough for him to understand not to answer. Explaining that Charlie was

Jack's son would also involve explaining that Mrs Moon was Emma, which Stella knew would be too distressing for Lucy right now.

'He used to be the gardener here.' Stella hesitated. 'He knew about the time tunnel and Harry disappearing to see Emma…

'Harry belonged to an old lady called Margaret who used to live here,' Stella went on, 'then one day he never came back. That's when Charlie moved away.'

'What about the old lady?' said Lucy.

'She died peacefully,' said Stella with a quick smile. 'She was very sweet and *very* old.' Stella flashed Tom another warning glance.

'She died in her sleep,' said Tom, staring at the ground in front of his feet.

Hannah bit her fingernail, casting her mind back to the muddled messages Stella had sent her while she was still in Hong Kong, and which were suddenly all making sense.

'Anyway, Tom's right,' Stella went on. 'At least Charlie won't think our story is bonkers — and he might have some ideas to help us.' She sighed. '*If* we can find him, that is.'

'Exactly,' said Tom, perking up. 'Come on, Stell, let's look online.' Stella and Hannah both pulled out their phones. 'Try *Charlie Green Gardener Kilburn,*' said Tom. 'That's where he moved to, remember. It's not that far away. Henry Wong comes on the bus to school from there.' Tom manoeuvred behind Stella, who was already typing into her phone.

'What do you mean *online?*' said Lucy.

'Like this!' said Hannah with a smile, and she held up her phone to show Lucy the Google page.

'But that's a telephone, not a *laptop*,' said Lucy, overemphasising the 'p' each time.

'Aye, but it's a computer too. Kind of like a miniature laptop.' said Hannah. 'It all comes from *the Cloud*,' she added, with a quick smile. 'If you sit behind me, you can watch.' Then she began tapping the phone screen.

'Errrr! This is hopeless!' Stella blew her cheeks out with a sigh and lay back on the mound. They'd spent 15 minutes searching every combination of Charlie Green, Charles Green, C Green and 'gardener' or 'gardening'. Even the online phone directory, where you got three free searches before having to pay, brought back nothing. No Charlie Greens anywhere near Kilburn or its NW6 postcode advertising gardening.

'Maybe he's retired,' said Tom. 'He said something about getting old.'

'He also said something about *working* closer to his home,' said Stella.

'He might not advertise even if he is working,' said Hannah, finally abandoning her search. 'Perhaps he just helps his neighbours.'

Lucy had been frowning, clearly deep in thought, for the last few minutes as she picked at the buckle at the back of her sandals. 'Are they sore?' said Stella, sitting up on her elbows.

'Oh, no. They're fine, thank you,' said Lucy. 'But I was just thinking about what Hannah said. In my time, you have to be quite rich to put advertisements in the newspapers about your work. Most people who work locally have little messages in shop windows or they get their work by just asking around and then people get to know them. Do they ever do that now? Shop messages, I mean?'

'Sure they do!' said Hannah. 'I'm always seeing postcards about babysitting in our newsagent — and other stuff.'

'In that case,' said Stella, sitting up. 'We'll have to go to Kilburn!'

'*How?*' said Hannah.

'On the bus, of course!' said Tom. 'Henry Wong said it takes half an hour, but I bet it's quicker at weekends.'

'You've got your bus pass, right, Han?' said Stella

quickly. Hannah nodded. 'Okay. I have my pocket money, so I'll pay for Lucy.'

As they walked from the main gardens into their patio garden, Stella crossed her fingers behind her back. 'We're just going to the high street, Mum. Hannah wants to window shop for her birthday outfit.'

In fact, the map app showed it as Kilburn High Road, but she felt that 'going to the high street' was general enough to cover her if they needed to explain themselves later. There was also a Fashion Max outlet store there, a favourite place to shop for clothes — another back-up reason for their visit.

'I'm going too!' said Tom brightly.

Stella's mum, who sat at a small table reading a paper in the dappled morning sunlight, looked up and pushed her sunglasses onto her head. 'Er, Stella. You're to keep Tom with you at all times. And make sure your phones are on. Hannah and Lucy — are your parents okay with you getting the bus down?'

'Of course,' said Hannah. 'I get the tube to school now.' She then poked Lucy in the back.

'Oh, they're absolutely fine about it!' said Lucy with a smile. 'I get the tube to school too.'

'Well, text me when you're there and when you're

on your way back, Stella. Enjoy — and no going off, Tom!' She then went back to reading her paper.

'Okay,' said Stella. 'Google Maps says it's the 23 from Blenheim Crescent around the corner for five stops, then the 316 to Brondesbury Road. Then it's a one-minute walk. Should take 25 minutes.'

In the short walk from the house to the bus stop, Lucy twisted her head left, right, up and down, periodically gasping and sighing as she took in the sights, sounds and smells of this familiar but different world. Sleek cars of all shapes, sizes and colours, and with fat tyres, whisked down streets whose buildings she recognised from her own time, but which had been magically transported to a new world where people talked on phones as they walked and wore light, unfussy clothes. No one wore hats and ladies' hair was free and flowing. Everything felt faster and more colourful. Not a horse or carriage in sight. No straw or horse manure cluttering the roads. And no boy sweepers ready to earn a penny to clear the way for pedestrians.

A low rumble above made her look up. 'What's *that?*' she shrieked, eyes like saucers as she cupped both hands over her head.

'An aeroplane,' said Tom with a grin. 'Dad went on

one to New York yesterday. It only takes seven hours.'
He glanced sideways at her mischievously as her mouth
fell open.

'Don't worry. You'll get used to them,' said Hannah
brightly.

Lucy gazed at the sky, slowly shaking her head.

A red double decker bus appeared around the
corner and came to a halt in front of them. The doors
concertinaed open with a hiss and clatter, causing Lucy
to step back in alarm.

'*Eeek!*' screeched Hannah, as Lucy landed on
her toe.

'Oh, I'm so sorry!' said Lucy, glancing back.

'No worries!' said Hannah. She smiled and nudged
her forward behind Stella, who had bleeped her pass
and was paying for Lucy.

'Upstairs!' said Stella, pointing to the ceiling, as the
doors hissed again then thudded shut behind them.

By the time they reached Kilburn High Road, 20
minutes and one bus change later, Lucy felt she was
beginning to acclimatise to her new surroundings —
the endless stop, start and noise of the traffic; the warm
fumes in her nose; the traffic lights that changed from
red to orange and green and back, as if by magic, and
which reminded her of the boiled sweets that she and

Emma so loved; finally, the people of all colours, shapes and sizes thronging the pavements.

'Okay. It's busier than I thought,' said Stella. 'Hannah, why don't you and Lucy start on this side? Tom and I will cross over. We need to check every window where we see postcard signs. If in doubt, take a photo — even if you can't read the name properly.'

'Good plan,' said Hannah.

'Call me if you find anything and I'll do the same.' Stella smiled at Lucy, whose eyes continued to dart all round. 'Are you okay?'

'I'm fine. Just trying to remember it all for Emma!'

'Quick, lights have changed.' Stella grabbed Tom's arm and stepped onto the zebra crossing.

Hannah and Lucy, and Stella and Tom made their ways up opposite sides of the High Road, stopping wherever they saw postcards advertising services in the window. There were far fewer such windows than they'd expected, on account of so many large shops, but always a lot of cards to check where they did find them — and some so annoyingly high they were difficult to read. To try to save time, Tom read the lower ones and Stella the higher ones.

After 15 minutes, a growing empty feeling told Stella this was a waste of time. She glanced across the road, scanning left and right, but Hannah and Lucy were nowhere to be seen. In panic, she tapped to call Hannah, who picked up right away, her voice drowned out by the sound of a passing bus. Stella let out a silent breath. 'Where are you? Have you found anything?'

'Nope.' Hannah replied, half shouting against the traffic noise. 'We're opposite Boots — where are you?'

'Okay — we're about ten metres farther on. Have you seen any signs for gardeners?'

'Nope! Lucy's been looking for handyman signs, too. No Charlies and no Greens.'

At that moment, Stella's phone pinged with a text. 'Hang on.'

How are you all doing?

She put her phone back to her ear. 'Eeek! I forgot to text Mum!' She glanced farther up the road. 'We're nearly at the end. There's a Spar supermarket on a corner. We'll wait for you there, then we'd better go back.' Stella ended the call and texted her mum back.

Sorry forgot! All fine! Going for ice creams soon. Back in about an hour. xx

Lucy's cheeks looked pale, and her eyes tired as she and Hannah crossed the road to join Stella and Tom. 'I'm sorry,' said Stella, reaching out to give Lucy a hug. 'It was worth a try, though. We'd better go back.'

'Let's get an ice cream,' said Tom, pointing to a small café about 15 metres away down the side street.

'Just what I told Mum!' said Stella. The relative quiet of the leafy road looked inviting after the bustle of the high road, and there were tables and chairs they could sit on outside.

'I'm sure we'll work something out,' said Hannah softly. She gave Lucy a warm smile, then linked arms with her.

As they left the noise of the street behind, thoughts and questions swirled in Stella's mind. Something in her bones told her Lucy couldn't have found her way here for no reason. And, as Lucy had said to them herself last night, the moles seemed to have appeared just when they were most needed. It *had* to be a sign, and there *had* to be a way they could get help for Emma. She let out a frustrated sigh as Tom bagged a seat at one of the two pavement tables.

'Okay. What do you all want?' she said, pointing at the sign.

'Chocolate ice cream with toffee nut sauce!' said Tom. He smiled and licked his lips.

Stella rolled her eyes. 'Too expensive, Tom. I'll get you a chocolate cone.' Tom frowned, then twisted his face into a wonky smile.

'Strawberry cone,' said Hannah. 'Would you like to

try one, Lucy? It's like ice cream sitting in a cone shape made of, er…' She smiled and bit her lip.

'Biscuit?' said Tom.

'Aye, something like that,' she replied with a quick sideways glance.

'Actually, we call them *cornets*. Yes, please,' said Lucy. 'Emms and I love strawberries, and we love ice cream.' She stared vacantly at the tabletop as her voice trailed off. Hannah reached across and rubbed her shoulder.

'It'll be okay,' she said with a smile.

As Stella entered the café, the clatter of cutlery in the back kitchen mingled with classical music being piped from a speaker somewhere nearby. Her eyes took a moment to adjust to the indoor light, then her heart quickened as she spotted a cork noticeboard crowded with postcards and small flyers on the wall opposite the counter. She stared over at it, trying to make out its contents.

'What'll it be, love?' Stella started and turned around. The elderly woman behind the counter wasn't much taller than she was. She had brown skin, a dusting of silver-grey afro hair, cheeks as round as apples and a friendly smile. Stella placed the order, then went over to study the board. She scanned up and down, down and up, willing a sign to appear — but there was nothing. She puffed her cheeks out and sighed.

'Here's your first two, love.' The lady handed two strawberry cones to Stella. She took them outside and returned for her and Tom's orders. As she walked back inside, and as the lady was scooping the chocolate ice cream into Tom's cone, the silhouette of a tall, slightly stooped figure appeared in the doorway at the far end of the room behind the counter. Stella jerked to a halt as her pale blue eyes met the familiar stare of Charlie Green.

13

A SURPRISE DELIVERY

'Is that you, Stella?' Charlie Green walked out from the doorway, his initially vacant stare dissolving into a warm smile. 'Well, *I'll* be—'

'This young lady a friend of yours, Charles?' said the lady with a wink as she placed a second cone, this time vanilla, into the stand in front of Stella.

'He used to be our gardener,' said Stella, her cheeks reddening.

'Oh, you're the young lady from Notting Hill way?'

'*Charlie!*' Tom stood in the doorway, eyes wide.

'Goodness, Charles, I never knew you'd made so many friends in those gardens!' said the ice-cream lady. Her tiny mouth curled up into a smile. 'Here, I'm guessing this one's yours, dear.' She picked out the chocolate cone from its stand and handed it across the counter to Tom.

'Oh, um, thank you.' Tom took the cone and began licking at the ice cream, his eyes fixed on Charlie Green.

'Actually—' Stella started. But Charlie Green interrupted her.

'Well, this is *quite* a coincidence.' He turned his head slightly and winked out of the lady's eyeline. 'Just this morning I was tellin' Polly here I had something to deliver to you from old Mrs Moon's solicitors.'

'Mrs Moon?' Stella let out a whispered gasp.

'Seven months it's taken to sort out her estate an' only yesterday I got a package with strict instructions to hand deliver to Stella Hawken. There I was all set to come out this afternoon, and here you are turning up in Kilburn! How on earth did you find me?' He winked again, still out of Polly's sightline.

'We didn't—' Stella's phone pinged. She looked down.

Sure you don't need collecting? Mxx

'Sorry! That's mum.' She texted back.

It's fine. Hannah just trying dress. Back in 30. xxx

'We just stopped for an ice cream!' said Tom. 'We'd been looking for y—'

'—for a dress in Fashion Max for my friend Hannah,' cut in Stella, twisting to glare at Tom.

Another customer came in whistling, stepping

around Tom in the doorway, then falling into conversation with Polly.

'Well, good for you, Tom, accompanying the ladies,' said Charlie with a chuckle. 'Now, wait there, Stella, and I'll fetch the package.' He paused and glanced back. 'There's one thing I need to explain to you, mind.' He then winked. Just before he turned away, Stella thought she caught a fleeting look of sadness in his eyes but couldn't be sure.

'You wait outside, Tom,' Stella said quickly. She lowered her voice, glancing at Polly, who was still chatting. 'Don't say anything until I come out.'

Charlie re-emerged from the kitchen and walked around the counter as Polly continued chatting with her customer. 'Over here, Stella,' he said, glancing at a small table in the back corner.

'Now,' he said, keeping his voice low and glancing occasionally in Polly's direction. 'I really don't know how you found your way here today of all days, but let's not waste time wi' that — them moles move in mysterious ways, as we know.' He pushed the blank white envelope he'd been holding across the table. 'This is for you.' He flicked another glance up at Polly. 'You'll find two things inside. A letter to me from Margaret Moon, and something she wanted me to pass on to you — I can't say I fully understand it, but bein' as you've turned up here, I expect it might make sense to you.'

Stella's breathing quickened. 'Emma's ill — her friend Lucy is here.' Tears welled in her eyes. 'That's why we were looking for you—'

Charlie's eyes widened. 'Well, now,' he breathed, 'that might explain it…' He slowly shook his head as he stared at the envelope for a moment, then looked up and pressed his lips into a smile. 'Time certainly moves in strange ways, that I will say.' He darted another glance at Polly, whose customer was just leaving. A look that hovered between fear and sadness flickered in his eyes, and he leant in a little farther. 'If you do go back,' he whispered, 'there's something else you must be prepared for. You'll need to stay strong.' He smiled, almost apologetically. 'I think Margaret was trying to remember it in her letter—'

'You all sorted over there with your board meeting?' Polly called with a laugh.

'Remember. Stay strong,' whispered Charlie as he stood up. 'We most certainly are,' he replied to Polly, his voice upbeat. 'That's my part of the job done — and Stella's saved me a trip!'

As Stella picked up the envelope, her phone pinged again.

Ok. See you soon. There's pasta here. Mx

Why did her mum always sign off 'M' when it was obvious the messages came from her? She smiled briefly, trying to ignore the butterflies now stirring in her tummy. What exactly was in the letter, and why did she need to *stay strong*?

'Thank you, Charlie. I'll study this when we get home,' she said out loud. She placed the white envelope into an inner zipped compartment of her small rucksack. 'Oh!' She reddened as they approached Polly. 'My ice cream! *And* I need to pay!'

'On the house, dear,' Polly said with a smile, handing her the vanilla cone, which had started to drip. 'And you're welcome anytime! Rain or shine, we always have ice cream! Here, take our card.'

Charlie nodded as she turned to leave. 'Safe trip back!' he called, with a wink.

'What's happened?' said Lucy, just finishing her ice cream. For the last few minutes she'd been lost in her thoughts, starting to worry about Emma and Sophie again, and wondering if this trip hadn't been the hugest mistake after all. And when Tom had reappeared, he'd sat frowning, acting most oddly, which had made her all the more anxious. Hannah, meanwhile, had been absorbed looking at her phone and giggling occasionally.

'Wait 'til we're on the bus,' said Stella with a broad grin. 'You're never going to believe this!'

· · ·

'What does it say, Stell?' Tom and Hannah reached over from the seat behind Stella and Lucy, vying for head space. Lucy's eyes darted back and forth between the emerging envelope and the front row view. The rest of the top deck was empty.

'We're about to find out!' said Stella, holding the blank envelope aloft dramatically. Her pale blue eyes flickered in the dappled sunlight as the bus passed along the tree-lined avenue. She quickly broke the seal at one end and reached in and pulled out a further envelope, which clearly contained some sort of package. On the front, the typed words *CHARLIE GREEN — CONFIDENTIAL* had been crossed out and underneath, in strong ballpoint pen, it read '**Stella Hawken - Confidential**'.

'That's Charlie's handwriting,' said Tom 'I recognise it from last year.'

'Yep!' said Stella. 'Okay, let's see what's in here.' The bus pulled to a sudden halt at some traffic lights, then lurched forward as Stella pulled back the seal. Peering inside, she could see a small box and a folded note. She pulled out the note and flicked it open against her chest, then glanced back to make sure no one was there. Then, as she held it out to read, Lucy, Tom and Hannah leaned inward — eyes still, lips slightly parted — waiting to hear.

. . .

Stella glanced to the end. *'It's from Mrs Moon,'* she whispered. And then she read.

Charlie — I found these tablets this morning and they rang a distant bell. I think you might need them. They're left over from that chest infection I had last month. I now remember the doctor gave me extras as back-up, but I didn't need them. I don't understand why, but I think Stella might come for them one day. Something to do with the time tunnel? Oh, how I wish my memory wouldn't play tricks on me!

Please don't give them to anyone but Stella and make sure she knows they were prescribed FOR ME and no one else. I think that's important. She seems sensible and I am sure knows that medicine is only for the person it is prescribed for. But please pass this note to her so I'm certain she understands.

I think there's something else important too about water, but I just can't remember.

If I have this all wrong, return them to the chemist or dispose of them safely.

Thank you for being there all these years. M

'Oh, my,' breathed Hannah. 'This must be the medicine we need!' She beamed at Lucy, who sat, eyes wide and vacant, calmly taking in what she'd just heard.

'And it's actually *her own*!' said Stella.

Stella glanced at Lucy, realising Lucy had just worked out that Mrs Moon was Emma. She reached for Lucy's hand, which lay limp in her lap. 'Are you okay? I'm sorry I didn't tell you—'

Hannah put her hand to her mouth. 'Oh, I'm *so* sorry,' she whispered from behind. The word *so* hung in the sudden silence.

Lucy pressed her lips together and looked out of the window, as if to take in the view. After a few moments, she breathed in deeply and turned to Stella, Hannah and Tom, eyes shining, but with a smile. 'I'm fine, actually. I think this *must* mean Emms is going to be all right!'

As Stella reached back into the envelope for the little box, the bus halted and a group of teenagers joined the top deck behind them. 'We'll check it later,' she said, and quickly put the envelope away.

Tom, suddenly feeling hungry, sat back in his seat, frowning. What was the water thing all about?

14

A MIDNIGHT WAIT

'Mum, can Lucy stay another night?' Stella crossed her fingers as she leaned over the bannisters at the top of the stairs. As she waited for the reply, she twisted and grimaced at Lucy, Hannah and Tom who stood in her bedroom doorway, faces expectant. She had planned to ask during lunch earlier but chickened out, deciding it would be easier from a distance, in case any awkward questions were asked.

'What about your homework?' her mum called up.

'All done! Same for Lucy. Her mum says it's okay.' She hated telling white lies, but this was a life and death emergency.

'All right. What about Hannah? If Lucy doesn't want to top and tail, there's the blow-up bed—'

'She has to go back. Her mum's coming.'

'Okay. That's fine, dear.'

'Yess!' said Stella, punching the air.

As they returned to her room, she could see that Hannah was putting on a brave face. Her grandparents were due that evening and there was no way she couldn't be there.

'Okay, let's check what's in the medicine box,' said Stella. She retrieved the envelope from where she'd hidden it under her pillow when they'd got back, then pulled out the box. Carved in biro onto one side was a note in Charlie's handwriting, which she read out loud **'Keep safe. See note.'** She turned the box over. Centred on the front was a printed label with medical wording, and above it the words *'Née Emma Gladstone'* in what Stella guessed must be Mrs Moon's handwriting.

'What does *that* mean?' said Tom, frowning.

'It's her maiden name,' said Lucy with a smile. *'Née* means 'born' and the extra 'e' is feminine because she's a girl. I learnt about it with Miss Cowley last month. She's my new governess. Mama's *desperate* for me to speak French!'

Hannah, Stella, and Tom stared at Lucy, mesmerised by the rhythm of her words. A brief silence followed.

'Yeah, but what's a maiden name?' said Tom, narrowing his eyes.

Hannah bit her lip and glanced at Stella, who

raised her eyebrows and grimaced because she'd forgotten.

'It's a girl's last name before they get married!' Lucy brushed a strawberry blonde ringlet from her face and smiled. '*Boys* don't have them, of course.'

'Exactly!' said Hannah with a sideways glance at Tom, which made Stella giggle.

'Okay. I'm going to Google the medicine,' said Stella, peering at the label. She picked up her phone. 'Here, someone read it out to me.'

'I'll do it.' Lucy took the box and read out each letter as Stella tapped into her phone: '*P-H-E-N-O-X-Y-M-E-T-H-Y-L-P-E-N-I-C-I-L-L-I-N*' As she reached the end, she let out a breath.

'Whaaa!' said Hannah. 'I wonder who invents these words?'

'Doctors!' said Tom with a grin.

'I've got it!' Stella turned her phone sideways and zoomed in. 'Pheno... Phenoxy-methyl-*blah blah* is a type of penicillin. It's an antibiotic used to treat bacterial infections, including ear, chest, throat and *skin infections*. It can also be used to prevent infections if you have sickle cell disease... blah blah.. or if you have your spleen removed.'

Everyone paused for thought.

'What's a spleen?' said Tom.

The children all exchanged glances, but no one replied.

'Let's see what else it says.' Lucy held up the box so they could all see.

Phenoxymethylpenicillin
Mrs Margaret Emma Moon. 30 March 2011.

For adults and children over 12 years take 2 x 250 mg tablet 4 times a day.
For children under age 12 take 1 x 250 mg tablet 4 times a day.
Take with water. Do not chew.
Batch Expiry Date: October 2014

'Phew! They're in date!' said Stella. She took the box from Lucy and pulled out two blister packs and did a quick count. 'Okay, these are all 250g and there's four rows of seven tablets in each pack. So 28 tablets per pack.'

They all looked at the dosage instruction again.

'It says four tablets a day for a child under 12,' said Lucy. 'Emma's not 12 until September.'

'Good!' said Stella. '4 x 7 makes 28 a week, so there's an extra week's supply if she needs it.'

'That's a *lot* of tablets,' said Hannah, eyes wide.

'Fingers crossed she won't need the second week,' said Stella.

The doorbell rang and voices echoed from downstairs.

'Hannah! your mum's here!'

Stella hurriedly reinserted the tablets, closed up the box, and put everything back under her pillow. 'We're just coming!'

Hannah sighed and picked up her rucksack. 'So, what are you going to do now? I *so* wish I could be there!'

'Wait for the moles, I guess.' Stella glanced at Lucy. They'd been so busy trying to get the medicine, they'd not had time to discuss their plan. Stella pulled at a lock of her white-blonde hair and stared out towards the gardens. In the back of her mind, she'd supposed the moles would just magically appear for them. But now she stopped to think, there was no guarantee. She and Tom knew all about them *not appearing*, that was for sure. Then what?

'I know they'll appear,' said Lucy. 'I just know it!'

'Hannah!'

Hannah stepped forward and hugged Lucy. 'It was *so* nice meeting you. I really hope Emma gets well again. And that I'll see you again?'

'Me too,' said Lucy. 'Thank you for being so kind.'

'Last call for Hannah! *Taxi's going!*' called Mrs Hawken, as Stella opened the door.

'Good luck!' whispered Hannah and blew them all kisses, then turned and ran down the stairs, her rucksack and braids bobbing on her back.

* * *

Stella had agreed with Tom she would knock for him when the house was quiet.

'Even if I'm asleep!' he had insisted.

'Promise!' she had replied. Leaving him behind wasn't an option. They were all in this together. Besides, Lucy had already told them about the clothes she'd hidden for them both. To leave him behind would be unthinkable. And, if she was honest with herself, she felt nervous about going without him.

She had switched off the lights by the time her mum popped her head around the door just after 11 p.m. and lay whispering with Lucy for the next half hour, moonlight seeping in through the wooden slats of the shutter. Lucy had retrieved her clothes from the bottom of the wardrobe and had them ready under the zed bed to change into if the moles appeared. Stella had her phone, a bottle of water and snacks and the medicine box safely stashed in her little rucksack, along with her notebook and a pencil.

It was just before midnight when the door creaked open and Tom tiptoed in. 'Tom! What are you doing?' squealed Stella in a whisper. 'I said I'd come and get you!' In that moment, she saw that Tom was dressed already and had his drawstring rucksack with him.

'Mum's asleep!' he whispered back crossly.

'How do you know?'

'She's snoring!'

'Are you sure?' Stella leapt out of bed and tiptoed to the door and out onto the landing towards her parents' bedroom. Their mum always left their bedroom door ajar when their dad was away. Stella let out a breath and crept back to her room. Tom was right. 'Okay. You're on mole watch while we get changed!' she said.

'This feels so strange,' whispered Lucy, looking down at her coat. It suddenly seemed to go on forever, its weight pulling her down, and her legs felt hot in her woollen stockings. She'd been away for no more than 36 hours, yet it somehow felt a lifetime.

'At least you'll be warm!' said Stella with a smile. Like Tom, she wore jeans, a T-shirt and a jumper and a lightweight jacket. They'd agreed what to wear and bring earlier, spurred on by Lucy, who told them *if you fail to plan, you are planning to fail.*

'Mama says it all the time — it's from Benjamin Franklin, one of the *founding fathers* of America,' she had

120

said dramatically. 'Mama says he was very clever and very kind and she wishes there were more politicians like him today.'

Bringing snacks along had been Tom's idea, remembering how hungry they'd been waiting for the moles last time. He had Benjamin Franklin to thank for that, at least.

For the next half hour, Stella, Tom and Lucy stood on Stella's small balcony looking out to the gardens — searching for any sign of movement. Small white clouds laced the night sky, backlit by the moon as it dipped in and out of view between and behind them. The trees and bushes swayed in a gentle breeze.

'Look how fast the moon's moving,' whispered Tom, scanning the sky.

'That's the clouds, silly!' said Stella. She glanced sideways with a giggle.

'*There!*' Lucy cut in, with a whisper, pointing to the left of a group of bushes about 20 metres away. Tom and Stella followed her gaze to a small clearing, but whatever it was had vanished. Lucy frowned. 'I could have *sworn!*'

At that moment the moon appeared from behind another cloud, lighting up the clearing, then disappeared again, casting it back into shade.

'Moon shadows,' said Stella. She blew out her cheeks and sighed.

'No! *There!*' squealed Tom.

Stella and Lucy glanced in the direction he was pointing, farther off to the left, to see a group of moles scuttling in a circle in the moonlight before vanishing.

'Now!' whispered Stella. 'Let's go!'

15

SOPHIE ON THE ISLAND

'*O uch!*' Sophie snatched her hand back from the branch she'd just reached onto and sucked at her finger. The taste of warm blood told her she'd cut herself. She wiped her hand on her coat and called up one last time. 'Lucy! Where *are* you?' Only the gentle rustle of leaves answered.

Blinking rapidly, she looked all around at the moonlit leaves and branches that surrounded her. 'I can't believe it!' she whispered. Angry tears filled her eyes as she began her descent.

She jumped the last few feet to the grass below, landing awkwardly on one ankle. 'Owwwch!' she squealed again. Then louder — 'OUCH! OUCH! OUCH!' Rubbing her ankle as she lay on the ground, she suddenly felt better, as if she'd just let go of something. She sat up and looked out across the lake beyond the small boat and took a deep breath. Then she dropped her head to her chest and burst into tears.

As Sophie's tears started to dry, she looked up. She stared at the boat in the moonlit water, still trying to work out what she'd been crying about. Was it being abandoned here on her own? Being tricked by Lucy? Or something more?

The bushes rustled, making her jump. As she put her hand to her chest, she pictured Emma alone in her bed with the fever. Tears welled again. Doctor Abbotts said it was to do with her leg, but that didn't make any sense. Cuts don't give you a fever — she knew that much. She blinked again, opening herself up to a thought that had been nagging at the back of her mind these past few days. She and Emma had been walking in the gardens the day before Emma's fall when a heavy rain shower came from nowhere. They'd rushed back to the house and Sophie had locked her out for a joke. It was only for ten minutes, and Miss Walker had reprimanded her when she came looking for them. Emma was soaked, and they'd needed to draw a hot bath for her. But she seemed fine afterwards and said it was fun. But chills took a few days to come out, didn't they?

She then thought back to Emma's fall the next day,

and all the fussing around when she'd had to stay in bed for her cut leg. She'd been in to see her, but not as often as she should have done, and even then she'd cheated on her at snakes and ladders after Emma had beaten her at Fishpond. Her cheeks burned, and a dark feeling came over her, as she pictured Emma's puzzled face when she'd told her the dice had landed on six and not four. She sniffed deeply and wiped her eyes and cheeks. Why did there always seem to be a little voice egging her on to be nasty to Emma?

The bushes rustled again. She jumped up in panic and looked up at the tree, but there was no sound. Then a thought struck her. Maybe Lucy was hiding in the shed? Perhaps this was all a trap to punish her for being so mean to her sister? She set off down the moonlit path to find her.

Of course, the shed was empty when she got there. *Where are you, Lucy?* she whispered to herself. A shiver ran through her. *I'm...* She paused and frowned, remembering the bag. What was in it, anyway? She opened the shed door again and pulled out the hoe, then went around the back. She breathed in deeply, mustering her courage as anger returned. Enough was enough. If Lucy was going to abandon her here as some kind of joke, she would dig up the bag and take it back. Two could play at that game — if she set her mind to it, perhaps she could row back across the lake after all. She raised the hoe and began scooping up the loose earth.

* * *

Stella, Lucy and Tom made their way on tiptoe downstairs — Lucy carrying her boots in one hand, Stella and Tom each with their rucksacks. They had left rolled-up towels from the landing cupboard underneath their duvets, just in case Mrs Hawken looked in during the night. With trainers and boots quickly on, they slipped outside and Stella clicked the kitchen door closed behind them. The patio gate squeaked loudly as Tom pulled it open. 'Quietly!' Stella mouthed, glaring at him in the moonlight.

'*Sorry,*' he whispered, baring his teeth in an awkward grimace. He held the gate open as Stella and Lucy passed through, then closed it by hand to prevent its usual 'clank.' The children hurried across the lawn in silence, towards the grassy mound that Stella and Tom called 'the Island'. Moments later, Stella flicked on her phone torch and they were scrambling inside the rhododendron bush that housed the time tunnel.

It took them a good half minute to locate the hole, and Stella was just starting to panic when her hand slipped over its lip. 'It's here!' she whispered. 'You go first, Lucy. I'll go in the middle and turn on my phone light. Tom, you follow me.'

Stella pushed her phone into her back jeans pocket with the torchlight facing outwards. As she had hoped, its ambient light was just strong enough to offer a glimpse of their immediate surroundings. The air was damp in her nostrils, and the ladder rungs cold and scratching against her palms. But it didn't matter — each new rung she passed took her closer to their goal of helping Emma.

When Lucy called up that she'd reached the tree, warmth flooded through Stella. It was as if she'd never been away. 'Hold on, Emma!' she said to herself. 'We're coming!'

'*Awesome!*' called Tom, his excitement plain to hear.

The children jumped down one after the other onto the moonlit lawn, breathless after their mad dash and downward climb. As they scrambled to their feet, Lucy stared at the lake. Something wasn't right. Her eyebrows knitted into a frown.

'Where's the boat?' said Tom.

'I... I don't know—' she gasped. She looked all around. 'Sophie? Are you there?' she called. '*Sophie!*' No reply. They walked to the edge of the lake — there was no sign of the boat.

Lucy breathed in and out, trying to gather her thoughts. If Sophie had gone back, she'd be waking the house right now. How on earth would she explain Stella and Tom? *'Quick!'* she cried in a whisper. 'We need to get you changed!' She turned and dashed down the path towards the shed, Stella and Tom behind her.

All three children stood staring at the dug-up hole. The hoe lay discarded to one side, piles of earth in every direction.

'She's taken them!' Lucy's voice trembled as she looked at the gap where the bag should be. Their only hope of a disguise was gone. Worse still, they were about to get turned in one more time by Sophie Gladstone. Why, *oh, why* had she brought her across here?

'Why would she do that when we're here to help Emma?' Stella stared at the hole, twisting a lock of her white-blonde hair around her finger.

'Because I left her behind!' said Lucy, her voice trembling. 'I didn't have a choice though, did I? The tunnel could've closed at any minute — I've never seen the moles dance that fast!' She breathed out with a sigh. 'Besides, Sophie thought I was talking nonsense when I said you were from the future. I don't think she'd have believed the time tunnel even if she'd *seen* it.' She stamped her foot, then pressed her fingers against her forehead. 'She's so jealous of Emms she can't see beyond herself! And even if she were here, I don't think she'd believe we have a cure.'

Stella breathed slowly in and out, trying to keep her thoughts clear, as much for herself as for Lucy and Tom. 'I think we should go back to the lake,' she said calmly. 'We need to make a plan to find a way over — *even* if it means swimming!'

Tom, trying to contain his despondence, nodded solemnly and took the lead back along the path. As he stepped into the opening, he took an inward breath and began running. 'It's an oar!' he called. He rushed to the bank and pulled it out at the paddle end, where it was lapping up against the bank in the moonlight.

Lucy's hand flew to her mouth. 'No!' she cried in a whisper. *'Please, no!'* The scene around her seemed to unfold in slow motion.

'What is it, Lucy?' Stella gripped her shoulders. Tom looked on in bewilderment. Neither was prepared for what came next.

'Sophie can't swim!' Lucy mumbled through sobs. 'This is *all my fault.*'

16

REFLECTIONS

It took Stella and Tom several minutes to calm Lucy. When she finally spoke, inward gasps for air punctuated her words, her chest rising and falling in shudders as she tried to catch her breath. 'Sh... She was afraid of the w... water. I persuaded her to come on the boat. I was af... afraid she'd go back and w... wake Mama.'

She put both hands to her face and started to sob again. Just as quickly, she dropped them and looked out across the water. 'Can you see the boat on the other side of the lake? Maybe she made it across?' Her voice was small, but suddenly held hope.

Tom, who had been scanning the far side of the lake, glanced at Stella and shook his head. A lump rose in Stella's throat. She swallowed hard. She had to stay strong for Lucy — and for Tom, but with every second that passed she felt her own strength slipping away. 'She might—'

A sound behind them made them start. They spun round. Sophie, white-faced, stood in the moonlight, her eyes wide with fright, drips of water falling from the hem of her long dark coat. 'I'm all right,' she whispered, her voice trembling. She let out a breath, then managed a half smile and looked down. 'My boots are ruined though.'

Lucy dashed forward. 'Oh, Sophie! Thank *goodness* you're all right!'

Sophie, who was a little taller than Lucy, dipped her head as Lucy flung her arms around her shoulders. For a few seconds Sophie's arms remained hanging at her sides, as if they belonged to someone else. Then, bit by bit, she raised them and returned Lucy's hug.

They quickly moved under the tree and sat down. 'Here,' said Stella, opening up her rucksack. 'Have a biscuit. It'll help with the shock.' It was a phrase borrowed from her mother — one she'd used countless times when they were younger to stem the flow of tears from whatever emergency had just occurred.

Sophie, who until now hadn't said anything more, fixed her gaze on the bright orange wrapper of the biscuit packet, which shone in the moonlight as Stella pulled it from her bag. 'In fact, I think we all need one of these.' Stella handed the biscuits out, reserving her widest smile for Sophie.

'Thank you,' said Sophie in a half whisper. She cocked her head to the side and frowned, staring at the writing on the packet. 'What does that say?'

'Hobnob! My favourite!' said Tom, taking a huge bite and consuming half the biscuit in one go, making Stella roll her eyes.

Lucy put her hand on Sophie's arm. 'Oh, Sophie. I really am *terribly* sorry. There's *so* much I need to explain. And to think on top of everything else you could have *drown*—'

'You don't need to,' said Sophie, her voice wavering. Her bottom lip wobbled. 'It's *my* fault.' She put her hand to her mouth as a tear rolled down her cheek. 'I was so worried about Emma, and all the time you were trying to help her. Have you *really* brought back a cure?' She looked around at the others, her eyes pleading.

Stella, Tom and Lucy exchanged surprised glances. 'So you *do* know about the time tunnel?' said Stella softly. She put her arm out, as if to reassure her.

Sophie nodded. 'Well, sort of — and the moles.' She turned to Lucy. 'I heard you just now behind the shed. I'm sorry for not believing you. And I think you're right. I've been a silly, jealous big sister.' Tears welled in her eyes. 'Emma would be all right if I hadn't—'

Lucy leaned forward and slipped her hand into Sophie's. 'It doesn't matter, Sophie. The main thing is that you're all right, and we can now *all* help Emms!'

'Now,' said Stella, 'the good news is, yes, we have a cure for Emma.' She cleared her throat. 'The bad news is we can't get across the lake, and Tom and I have no clothes to change into!'

Sophie gave a puzzled frown. 'Of course we can get across the lake!'

Stella, Lucy and Tom's eyes jumped wide.

'I only got three feet in before I changed my mind — the boat's round the other side of those bushes. It wouldn't go where I wanted it to, so I got out and pushed it back. It's really squidgy in the water by the bank!'

'What about the clothes?' said Lucy.

'They're still in the bag in the boat. I think that's what caused all the trouble — it kept rolling around, sending the boat in different directions.' Sophie paused and glanced around. 'But that's not why I came back.' She looked down at her lap.

'How do you mean?' said Lucy.

'Well, when I was fighting with the boat, I started thinking about what you'd said about children in the future and wondering if the clothes I found in the bag could be for them.' She paused again and gazed at the far bank. 'You know, I think I *could* have made it over if I'd really wanted to — but that's when I decided to hide and wait for you.' She turned and smiled at Tom and Stella. 'The oar must've slipped out of the boat. I honestly hadn't noticed.' She nibbled the edge of her biscuit and smiled. 'So, yes, I know about the time tunnel. And now I know about *Hobnobs!*'

It took Stella and Tom a good ten minutes and much huffing and puffing to get into the clothes that Lucy had brought for them. They packed their own clothes and rucksacks into the laundry bag and hid it under some tools in the shed. Stella retained a small drawstring pouch which she'd brought separately for her phone, notebook and pencil, and the medicine.

'How do I look?' said Stella, emerging through the shed door and twirling around in the long-sleeved pale blue muslin dress from the bag.

'It's a little short, but it will do,' Lucy said with a smile. Then her eyes widened as they fell on Stella's white trainers, which looked most odd with the black woollen stockings. 'I can't *believe* I didn't think of shoes,' she said, glancing around sheepishly. 'I'll find you some when we get to the house.'

Tom frowned as he paused in the shed doorway. 'I

think these are a bit long!' He stared down at the brown breeches, which flapped at his waist and almost reached his ankles.

'Here. If you roll from the waist, they'll come up shorter,' said Sophie, stepping forward to help him. 'That's better. Now they end just below your knee.'

'You look like a boy from a Charles Dickens novel!' said Stella with a giggle.

'Oh, Mama *adores* Charles Dickens books!' said Lucy. 'She said he always *roots for the underdog.*'

'What does that mean?' said Tom.

'He cares about the poor people,' said Sophie with a shy smile.

'Okay, we'd better make a plan,' said Stella.

Over the next ten minutes, during which Stella explained about sepsis and antibiotics to Sophie, and how Emma would need four tablets a day for a week, they batted around various ideas for reaching her.

Lucy told them about an *emergency mole hunt key* to Emma's back door that she and Emma had hidden in the garden. At first this had excited them, but each time they thought about how to use it, they came up against the same problem — how to get to her room every four hours without encountering one of the servants. More to the point, if she was asleep with a fever, how could they get her to take the tablet?

'There has to be something we're not thinking of,' Stella said with a sigh.

Then Sophie sat up. 'I could do it at night!' she said. 'I could start as soon as we get across. The servants will be in bed, and I know my way in the dark.' She peered into the distance, frowning, clearly working things out in her mind. 'At least it will get us started — and time *is* critical.' She glanced around at three smiling faces.

Stella took out her notebook and pencil from her pouch. *'If you fail to plan, you are planning to fail,'* she said with a sideways glance at Lucy. She then flicked on her phone torch, making Sophie gasp. 'Let's write everything down so we're sure it will work.' Then everyone chipped in as they crafted a *day one* plan based on Sophie's offer.

'We'd better get ready to go,' Stella said when the plan was as complete as it could be. 'We'll go over it one more time on the other side.' And they all scrambled to their feet.

17
THE NIGHT VISIT

They angled the boat bow-first to the bank. 'You first, Tom,' said Stella as she and Lucy each gripped one side to keep it from rocking. Tom crouched down and stepped in and sat to one side on the far bench seat, facing towards them.

'Okay, now you, Sophie.' Sophie hesitated, breathing deeply in and out of her nose as she looked into the well of the boat. Stella and Lucy exchanged glances, each realising just how brave Sophie had been even to think of trying to row across on her own earlier. Just as brave, Stella thought, to change her mind and stay to help them.

Sophie let out a final deep breath and stepped in, keeping low, then sat beside Tom at the far end. The boat sat firm in the water.

'I'll come last,' said Stella.

As Lucy's first foot landed in the boat, it tipped in a sudden jerk to one side, making Sophie cry out. Lucy quickly sat down on the middle bench, facing Tom and Sophie, and reached forward. 'It's all right,' she whispered, rubbing Sophie's arm.

The boat rocked again as Stella stepped in, but stabilised as she settled behind Lucy on the small seat in the boat's bow.

They had agreed that Lucy would row since she'd had more practice than Stella and Tom. Stella pushed them off, then Lucy manoeuvred them around until her back and the bow of the boat faced the far bank.

As the gentle splash of wood on water cut through the night air, Stella strained her neck, looking in all directions. The light of the moon, filtering down through the surrounding trees, cast a dappled path across the water to the far bank behind her — as if laid on just for them. Farther out, ribbons of silver danced on the surface between ominous black patches that looked like lakes within a lake. The surrounding bushes, nestled below tree trunks, were in darkness. She narrowed her eyes, trying to see if the crimson-pink azaleas were in bloom, then realised their buds would be closed at night. After last year's adventure, she had looked them up and now knew every last detail about their flowering habits.

A sudden flap of large wings through branches cut

through the night air, making everyone jump, and causing Lucy to lose her rhythm and the boat to rock violently. Sophie, lips pressed together and eyes darting wildly in all directions, gripped her side of the boat.

'What was *that?*' whispered Tom.

'Owl,' declared Lucy. She adjusted the oars and started rowing again. 'Emms and I have heard them lots at night.'

'Are you okay?' Stella leaned sideways to catch Sophie's eye from behind Lucy.

Sophie smiled and nodded, but her eyes still shone with fear.

'We're nearly at the other side,' said Tom, peering at the bank. 'You'll be fine, Sophie.'

'Okay,' said Stella, after they'd pulled up the boat and laid the oars back. 'Time to re-check our plan.'

'Over there,' said Lucy, pointing to a large log. 'This is where Emms and I meet for our mole hunts.' She smiled. 'Emms calls it the *Thinking Log.*'

As they all sat down, Stella pulled her notebook, pen and the little medicine box from her pouch and switched on her phone torch once more. This time, Sophie's eyes simply lit up in wonder.

'Right,' said Stella, putting on her best teacher's voice as she shone the torch on the open notebook.

'Think carefully and let me know if we've forgotten anything. Here goes:

'1: Stella, Tom and Lucy to go back to Lucy's house. Lucy has hiding place for us in a side room. Brackets — Lucy to find shoes.'

'You don't need to say *brackets*,' said Tom, frowning.

Stella narrowed her eyes at him, then smiled. She continued:

'2: Sophie uses Emma's hidden *emergency mole hunt key* to get into her own house. Lucy — are you sure it will be there?'

'*Yep!*' said Lucy, tasting the 'p' on her lips. She liked the way they said *Yep* in Stella's time and decided she might start trying it out. 'Under the large stone just outside your garden gate, Sophie.'

'3: Sophie visits Emma with our message and helps her take the first tablet. If possible, stays for four hours in own room to help with the second one. Then sneaks back out.'

Tom sighed and started shaking his head.

'*What?*' said Stella crossly.

'What if she's not on her own? How does *that* work?'

'Why didn't you say that before?' said Stella, glaring.

'I tried!' said Tom, his eyes suddenly smarting. They'd all been so excited and busy making their plan earlier, he'd found it hard to get a word in edgeways. Then he'd somehow forgotten about it.

'Actually, it'll be fine!' said Sophie, putting her arm out towards Tom. 'Emma has a night nurse sitting with her. She won't know I'm not staying in the house. I'll just say I want to see her. She's hardly going to stop me, is she? Anyway, she might be asleep!'

'Okay,' Tom whispered. He frowned and looked at his shoes. Butterflies and moths began stirring inside him as he realised just how easy it would be for Sophie to get caught.

'Sorry, Tom,' said Stella, her voice gentler. 'That was a good question.' She glanced back at her notebook and tapped her chin with her pen. 'Right, where was I?

'Ah, yes. 4: Sophie returns to Lucy's. *Brackets—*' She cleared her throat and flicked a glance at Tom. 'Um, Sophie returns to Lucy's. We have left kitchen door unlocked.

'5: Lucy smuggles breakfast upstairs and we, er — plan the next part of plan. Then we try to visit Emma.'

Stella closed her notebook and glanced around. 'Well, it's a start at least!'

'Perfect!' said Lucy. 'For the next bit, we'll just have to *cross that bridge when we come to it*, as Mama would say.'

'Are you sure your mum won't find us?' said Tom anxiously.

'Mama never comes into my room — oh, unless I'm ill, of course,' said Lucy brightly. Stella and Tom exchanged startled glances. 'It's mostly Nancy, our housemaid, for cleaning, and sometimes the housekeeper Mrs Dunford.' She flicked her strawberry blonde hair over her shoulder. 'Anyway, the room you'll be in is off the side and just has old luggage in it. No one ever goes in there — not even Nancy.' She giggled. 'I know because of the dust!

'Let's go!' she said, standing up. Her skin tingled and her heart felt warm — her plan was working. Finally, they were going to help Emma.

As they emerged from the wooded path that led to the lake, they all exchanged hugs with Sophie. 'Are you sure you'll be all right?' whispered Lucy. 'Remember, it's the large stone to the right of the your gate.'

'I'll be fine. If it goes wrong, I'll just say I came back because I was worried and used a spare key.' She smiled and patted Tom on his head, which made him frown slightly, then headed off across the moonlit lawn towards her house.

'Follow me,' whispered Lucy. 'Just remember to take off your shoes when we go in and carry them upstairs.' The first time she'd been on a mole hunt with Emma, she'd left muddy footprints up the stairs, which had taken very complicated explaining and a white lie that involved sleepwalking. She didn't want to have to go through *that* again — especially with three sets of footprints!

Lucy's house, which looked similar to Tom, Stella and Emma's house but wider, loomed over them in the darkness as they passed silently through its ornate back-garden gate. 'The door's unlocked,' Lucy whispered. A gentle breeze swayed the branches of the oak and plane trees in the gardens behind as they stooped to remove their shoes. As soon as they were inside, Lucy ducked into a side room and left her boots, then led them through a kitchen that Stella could see was far larger than Sophie and Emma's, and centred around two wooden tables rather than one. The shadowy outlines of pots and pans stacked on surfaces and hanging from the walls seemed to watch in silence as they passed through. As they emerged at the top of narrow stairs, Stella's eyes widened. A vast, shimmering chandelier hung over a hallway that seemed as grand as a living room. At the far end, to the right of the front door, a sweeping staircase led away with a curve to the upper floors.

Lucy turned and put her finger to her lips, then headed for the stairs.

. . .

Sophie quickly spotted the large stone as she approached her back gate. She paused and looked up, running her fingers around the box containing the medicine, which sat snugly in her coat pocket. The house was in darkness, aside from a faint flicker escaping through a crack in the shutters at Emma's bedroom window. The night nurse sat with a candle rather than use the electric lights. Sophie breathed out to calm herself. The fact that the nurse was there, still on duty, was good news.

She eased the stone up and retrieved the key, which lay, as Lucy had described, in a slight hollow, wrapped in cloth. Lucy had explained how Emma had found it in the well at the bottom of the steps outside the kitchen door the day after Stella, Tom and Lucy had broken in at night to rescue Jack — it must have fallen down there in all the commotion when Sophie had shouted the house awake. They called it the *emergency mole hunt key* in case anything went wrong when they were mole hunting and Emma got locked out. Sophie smiled. How clever her little sister was — if ever there was an emergency that needed that key, this was it.

Once inside, Sophie slipped into the boot room and removed her coat and boots, and the woollen stockings she'd put on under her nightdress to keep her warm

144

before following Lucy. She then tiptoed into the kitchen and dried her damp feet with a towel that hung beside the range. A low whine cut through the silence. She looked up, her heart thumping, to see Harry staring at her from his basket at the other end of the range. She froze, waiting for the barks. Miraculously, none came. *'Good boy, Harry!'* she whispered, letting out a breath. She tiptoed past him, heading for the stair door, then halted with a sigh. The tablets! She returned to the boot room and retrieved the pack from her coat pocket and tiptoed past Harry one more time, willing him to say quiet. He lifted his head and growled, then yawned and gave out a low whine before settling back down. Soon she was climbing the stairs.

Dim yellow light spilled out from under Emma's door. Sophie knocked gently. No reply. She grasped the door handle, eased it round and pushed the door open, just far enough to slip in. Emma lay fast asleep on her back, her face flush and moist in the candlelight, her dark curls damp and dishevelled, spilling onto the pillow around her. The night nurse sat in a rocking chair on the far side of the bed, a rug over her lap, eyes closed and mouth slightly open, as if paused in thought.

Sophie crept to Emma's bedside and knelt down out of view. She opened the end of the box and tipped the four tablets Stella had removed from the blister packs for Day 1 into her palm.

She glanced up to Emma's bedside table where a jug of water and glass sat, as they always did. Slowly, she knelt up beside Emma, the tablets warm in her palm. The night nurse hadn't moved. Emma's breath was gentle. Feeling tears welling, Sophie gently pressed her sister's shoulder. Emma frowned, her breathing quickening and becoming louder as she stayed flat on her back. Sophie darted an anxious look at the night nurse, who maintained her statuesque sitting pose.

'*Emma,*' whispered Sophie. '*Wake up! I've got a message from Stella and Tom!*' She pressed Emma's shoulder again, willing her to wake up. She tried again. '*Emma!*' With each second Emma slept on, Sophie's spirits sank further. Blinking back tears, she let out a shuddering sigh. Just then, Emma's eyes flicked open.

'*Stella?* Is that you?' she murmured in a whisper, staring at the ceiling. Then she twisted her head to meet her sister's gaze.

Sophie, cheeks burning, darted a glance towards the night nurse, who snorted and closed her mouth. Sophie snatched her hand to her mouth and pressed her forefinger to her lips. '*Shhh! No!* It's me — Sophie. But I've *seen* Stella. She's brought medicine for you!'

Emma's eyes jumped wide as a smile lit up her face. '*Oh, thank you, Stella! How lovely!*' she breathed. She turned fully towards Sophie and put her hand over her arm where it rested on the bed, then fell into a deep sleep.

The rocking chair creaked on the far side of the bed as the night nurse jolted awake to meet Sophie's panicked glance. 'Oh, dear me, now. You must be Miss Sophie. What *are* you doing in here at this hour? I really don't think—'

'No. It's fine,' said Sophie quickly. She fumbled as she slipped the pill box up her left sleeve. 'I'm worried about my sister. Please don't wake anyone. I just want to be with her.' Tears filled her eyes as she understood how true those words were. She dropped her chin to her chest. 'I can't bear to think of losing her. She's so funny, and so clev…' Her voice trailed off as she found the night nurse at her side.

'Here,' she said, pulling over a chair. 'You sit here, Miss Sophie. I'll not say a word. Seen too many lost to the fever, I 'ave. An' too many words of regret after. If you want to be with your sister, that's fine wi' me. Just don't you go telling on me to the housekeeper, eh? I'm Nurse Bagshaw by the way.' She winked down at Sophie and reached to help her up.

'Thank you so much!' said Sophie, rising from her knees and perching on the seat. She hesitated. 'How is she?'

The night nurse felt Emma's forehead with the back

of her hand. 'Still hot. Too, too hot,' she murmured, shaking her head. 'Doctor's back in the morning. Now you keep an eye while I go for more cold towels. I'll be back presently.'

'Of course,' said Sophie, holding back tears. She glanced back as the door opened. 'Oh, there's fruit and cheese in the pantry if you need something to keep you going. I'll watch over her.'

'Well, that's very kind of you, Miss Sophie. I'll be going down anyway. I won't be long gone. You come and find me, mind, if anything changes.'

'*Emma!* you need to wake up!' Sophie felt afraid and guilty for interrupting her sister's sleep — she looked so peaceful as she lay there. She put her arm on Emma's shoulder and rocked it gently. '*Emma!*' Emma's eyes flickered open again. She frowned.

'Is that you, Sophie? I was dreaming you were Stell—'

'*Yes!*' whispered Sophie. She gently grasped Emma's shoulder again. 'Can you *try* to wake up? Nurse will be back in a minute. *I've got important news.*' Emma blinked at her slowly, as if to prove she was properly awake.

'*What?*' she whispered.

'I've seen Stella and Tom *and they've brought medicine to make you better!*'

'*Stella and Tom? How?!*' She tried to push herself up to sit, but collapsed back down in a short coughing fit. Sophie glanced towards the door in panic, wondering if she should call the nurse.

'Oh, this *beastly* cough,' moaned Emma. '*How? Tell me*—'

'It was Lucy — she went through the time tunnel to get help.'

Emma gasped. '*Dear* Lucy! She told you? *The moles! I knew*—'

'Quick,' said Sophie. 'Nurse will be back soon.' She opened her palm and handed Emma one of the tablets. 'You need to take one of these every four hours with water. No chewing. You'll start to feel better after two days, and nearly back to normal after three days, but you *must* finish them all. That's very important, or it just comes back.'

'*I can't wait to see Stella!*' Emma said weakly.

'She can't wait to see you!' said Sophie. She reached for the glass of water on Emma's bedside and helped her sit up. Emma put the tablet into her mouth and took a large gulp of water. '*Done!*' she said with a smile and stuck her tongue out at Sophie. 'Oh dear,' she added, her eyelids drooping. 'I feel so tired'.

The landing clock on her fireplace struck twice, announcing 2 a.m.

'I'm coming back at 6 o'clock to help with your

second one, before everyone wakes up,' said Sophie. She pulled open the top drawer beside Emma's pillow and pushed the remaining three tablets into the back corner. 'If Mrs Howe stops me coming, the next three are in here.' She held up the little box and opened the second drawer down. 'The rest are in here at the back.' She pushed the box in and re-closed the drawer.

'I can't believ— oh, thank you, Sophie!' whispered Emma, snuggling down with a smile. *'You're the best.'*

Just as her eyes fluttered closed, the door opened.

'Everything all right?' asked Nurse Bagshaw, setting a china basin with damp towels on the side.

'She's still sleeping,' said Sophie, feigning a yawn. 'I think I'll go back to bed now, but I might come back early before everyone's awake. It's quite calming sitting alone with her.'

'You do as you like, Miss Sophie.' Nurse Bagshaw smiled, reaching for one of the damp towels she'd brought up. 'Though who's bettin' you don't sleep in after being up in the middle o' the night!'

Sophie crept to her bedroom, slipped into bed, and drifted in and out of sleep until the clock struck six. She then tiptoed back to Emma's room, where she found the nurse helping Emma back into bed.

'Well, if it isn't your big sister back to keep you company,' she chuckled. 'Miss Emma's just used the lavatory. You're lucky to find her awake.'

'Can I sit for a while?' asked Sophie.

'Just ten minutes. She needs all the rest she can get. Besides,' she flicked a glance at the fob watch that hung from her chest, 'the house is awake soon and we don't want Housekeeper catching us, do we now?' She adjusted her white cap and smoothed the front of her apron. 'Well, as you're here, I think I'll make me some tea. No excitement while I'm away, eh?' And with a nod and wink she was gone.

Emma's cheeks were still flushed as she lay back on her pillow. 'Oh, *dear* Sophie, I thought I'd dreamt you were here until nurse told me.' Her voice was tired and slow and hoarse. She hesitated and frowned. 'Did I *imagine*—'

'*No, you didn't!*' Sophie glanced quickly back towards the door. 'Stella and Tom are here, and we're going to get you better!'

'Oh, thank goodness!' Emma smiled and closed her eyes.

'*Don't go back to sleep!*'

'I'm not!' Emma blinked her eyes back open as Sophie pulled the drawer open and retrieved a tablet.

'It's every four hours, remember. That's one now and the next one at 10 o'clock.' Emma stuck out her tongue, ready to receive the tablet, then gulped from the water glass her sister passed.

'*Where are they?*' she whispered, stroking her throat to help the tablet on its way.

'At Lucy's. She's hiding them in a luggage room by her bedroom!' Sophie put her hand to her mouth and giggled. 'I'm supposed to be staying there too, but I sneaked out. Nurse thinks I'm staying here—'

At that moment, the door handle rattled.

'She's just having a drink,' said Sophie, nudging the drawer closed as the nurse entered.

'Excellent,' said Nurse Bagshaw with a smile. Her cup of tea rattled on its saucer as she carried it across the room towards a small table by the window.

'I'm so tired,' whispered Emma. She had started to curl a dark ringlet around her finger, usually a sign she was signalling a plan, but as her energy drained, her arm dropped. Something Sophie had just said about the time was important, but the words which she'd seen clearly in her mind's eye just a moment ago had skittered away, like leaves in a breeze.

'I'll come back later — maybe around 10 o'clock,' said Sophie to the nurse. She widened her eyes, trying to catch Emma's attention as her eyes flickered, but she was already falling back to sleep.

'Doctor Abbotts will be leaving around then,' said Nurse Bagshaw. 'Day visitors will be up to him, I'm afraid, Miss Sophie. Let's hope her temperature's no higher.'

'Please don't tell them I was here,' said Sophie.

'Of course not, Miss Sophie. You get some more sleep now.'

Moments later, Sophie was in the boot room, pulling on her coat and boots. Harry had simply looked up in silence as she had crept past him. She stuffed her half-dried stockings in her coat pocket and slipped out of the door, locking it behind her. Once through the back gate, she replaced the key under the stone and made her way across the gardens in the still, dawn air.

As she came closer to Lucy's house, she caught a movement out of the corner of her eye, close to one of the distant rhododendron bushes. She stopped and waited, flicking her glance sideways. All was still. She let out a breath and hurried on, hoping Lucy had remembered to leave the kitchen door unlocked. She descended the stairwell and turned the handle, breathing a sigh of relief as the door opened — then came face to face with Lady Cuthbertson and her housekeeper, Mrs Dunford, coats on, clearly on their way out. Beyond them, Lucy stood in her long white nightdress, eyes wide, slowly shaking her head.

· · ·

'Thank *goodness!* There you are, Sophie, dear!' Lady Cuthbertson stepped forward and pressed Sophie towards her in a hug, then stepped back, holding her at arm's length while looking her up and down. 'We were about to send out a search party! Where *have* you been, my dear?' She glanced down at Sophie's muddied boots and bare legs — and at the sodden tights that hung out of her coat pocket.

Sophie felt her cheeks drain as she scrabbled in her head for a story. 'Oh, dear, Lady Cuthbertson. I'm so very sorry. I… I…' She glanced at Lucy, who was gesticulating and mouthing something in the background, creating a walking sign with two fingers. Sophie refocused her gaze on Lady Cuthbertson. 'I've been for a walk in the gardens. I couldn't sleep. I'm so sorry to have troubled you.'

'Your boots are soaking, dear!'

'It's the dew. I had no idea—'

'My dear girl, we need to get those clothes off you right away. We can't have you catching a chill too. Mrs Dunford, can you please draw a hot bath for Sophie?'

'Right away, my lady.'

'*Now,* Sophie,' said Lady Cuthbertson, as she started to unbutton Sophie's coat, 'I know you're worried about your sister but—'

'Oh, I *really* am!' said Sophie, adding in extra drama for good measure, even though the statement was true. 'And it's so kind of you to have me to stay, but I think I'd rather be at the house so I can sit with her when she's asleep. Especially as Mama and Papa are away. Would it be *awfully* rude of me to ask to move back?' She flicked a glance at Lucy, who widened her eyes and nodded with approval.

Lady Cuthbertson smiled and put a hand on each of Sophie's shoulders. 'You may not believe it, dear, but I know *just* how you must feel.' She paused and sighed, her eyes suddenly glistening. 'Fevers are so unpredictable.' She bent her head and kissed Sophie on the top of her head. 'Doctor Abbotts is due back at your house this morning — let's see what he says later, shall we? But, whatever happens, please no more disappearing on us — your mama and papa would never forgive me if anything happened.'

'I'm sorry, Lady Cuthbertson.'

Lady Cuthbertson took Sophie's coat and put it over a chair beside the range. 'Lucy, back to bed now, dear. You too after your bath, Sophie. In fact, I think we could all use another hour's sleep!' As she led them towards the back stair, she began unbuttoning her own coat.

· · ·

'Sophie's back and she's given Emma two lots of medicine!' whispered Lucy, beaming, as she poked her head into the luggage room.

Stella and Tom lay top to tail under a blanket on a doubled-over eiderdown which they'd fashioned into a bed. Both items had come from a chest in Arthur's bedroom. A pair of Arthur's ankle boots sat against the far wall, tested and fitted, ready for use. None of Lucy's shoes or boots fitted Stella, but Lucy had told them they'd just have to *cross that bridge when we come to it*.

Stella, who had just dozed off, mumbled in her sleep.

'Awesome!' replied Tom. He'd found it impossible to fall asleep. His mind still buzzed at the prospect of meeting Emma and — he hoped — Jack again. He'd decided he would hold off asking about meeting Jack until Emma was better. Lucy had said he sometimes came to the gardens with his father, so surely they'd know where to find him.

'Oh,' Lucy added, almost as an afterthought. 'Sophie got caught!'

'Caught?' Tom sat up with a gasp.

'*Shhh!*' whispered Lucy. 'It's fine. She's having a bath and everyone's going back to bed. I'll bring you food in the morning.'

She glanced at a rose decorated chamber pot that she'd set discreetly at the far end of the room.

'Remember, you can use that if you're desperate. Otherwise, I'll sneak you back out to the lavatory when the coast's clear.'

'Yeah, right,' said Tom, grimacing.

As Lucy closed the door, he lay back down to try to sleep.

18

PROGRESS

The morning after Sophie's night visit, Mrs Howe, the housekeeper, and Miss Walker, the governess, stood at the foot of Emma's bed while Doctor Abbotts examined her. 'She's still not out of the woods, I'm afraid,' he said as he removed his stethoscope from her chest. 'Her heart rate's still high. However, there *may* be a chink of light as her temperature seems to have stabilised, so we have that to be thankful for — for now at least.' He eyed them in turn, his expression solemn. 'But fevers are unpredictable, as I'm sure you both know, and especially at night.' He opened his bag and dropped in the stethoscope. 'Ensure hourly checking during the day and keep her cool with moist towels. The night nurse will need to stay on, of course. Have you managed to get another telegram to Mr and Mrs Gladstone, Mrs Howe?'

'Not since the first one, I'm afraid,' she replied. 'It's impossible to get through — there's talk of heavy rain up where they're staying now.' She shook her head and sighed. 'Of course, there was no cause for worry in our first message. It was just a leg cut—' Her voice trailed off as Emma murmured and turned over. Mrs Howe stepped to the bedside and brushed Emma's dark ringlets from her cheek.

'Is that you, Sophie?' Emma murmured, her eyes flickering.

'No, Miss Emma, it's me, Mrs Howe.'

'*Oh,*' breathed Emma, then closed her eyes and began drifting back to sleep.

The doctor snapped his bag shut, starting her awake again. He pulled out his pocket watch. 'Goodness — 10 o'clock already! — I need to get on. Now, if you would see me out, Mrs Howe, I shall be back at the same time tomorrow. Telephone my office if you need me sooner.'

Emma dozed halfway between waking and sleep in the sudden silence. The voices that had echoed in her head moments earlier, along with the shadowy silhouettes at her bedside, had seemed to be part of a dream. But something had jolted her awake. Then the doctor's voice. *'10 o'clock already!'* Her eyelids were heavy as she tried to force them open. *10 o'clock.* Why did this seem familiar? Important even? She breathed out, feeling herself start to drift off just as the ring of the doorbell sounded in the distance downstairs. Her eyes snapped open. *Sophie's visit! The tablets!*

She blinked as she lay on her side, staring at the door. A shaft of sunlight spilled from the half-open shutters across the room and onto her bedside table. The drawer was at eye level. She reached out and pulled it open and felt around at the back. As she located one of the tablets, her heart fluttered. She *hadn't* imagined this. She quickly withdrew her hand, grasping the tablet between her thumb and forefinger, and nudged the drawer closed. Then she eased herself up to a half sideways sitting position and reached for the glass of water. At that moment, the door opened and Eliza, the housemaid, put her head in.

'Oh, goodness! You awake there, Miss Emma?' She darted across the room. 'Here.' She took the glass from Emma and set it on the side while she helped her into a full sitting position and placed a pillow at her back. 'That's better.' She picked up the glass and held it to Emma's mouth while she took a couple of sips.

'Thank you,' said Emma, clenching the tablet in her warm palm. Eliza set the glass back down. 'Actually,

I think I'll sit for a few minutes and look out the window. It's so *boring* sleeping.'

'Of course, Miss Emma. I hear your temperature has stabilised. That's a good sign if you ask me. Now, you just ring the bell if you need help. Mrs Howe will be in later.'

'Who was at the door?' said Emma as Eliza turned to leave.

Eliza smiled and hesitated. 'Just a delivery. Why, you expecting visitors?'

'I wouldn't mind,' said Emma, trying to hide her disappointment. 'Can you ask Mrs Howe if Sophie can come in to see me later?'

'Of course. Now, you get your rest. You'll be right as rain before you know it, and visitors coming out of your ears, I wouldn't be surprised!'

The moment the door clicked shut, Emma reached for the glass and put the tablet on her tongue, then swallowed it in one gulp. She then eased herself back down and was soon in a deep sleep.

In fact, when the doorbell had rung just after 10 a.m. it hadn't been a delivery. Not wanting to be overhead on the telephone, Lady Cuthbertson had come in person to relay news of Sophie's night walk and get an update on Emma. On hearing the news, Mrs Howe and Miss

Walker immediately agreed she should move back to the house for her own wellbeing, and that Miss Walker would go back to collect her. Eliza was under strict instructions not to mention anything to Emma about the night walk, for fear of stressing her.

'How strange,' Miss Walker said as she strolled with Lady Cuthbertson. 'She was so agitated at the house yesterday, I thought the change would take her mind off things.'

'I don't know. Young girls of her age can *change like the wind*,' said Lady Cuthbertson, glancing sideways with a smile. 'We've all been there! Anyway, she's been quite insistent she'd rather be close to Emma. It was all I could do to stop her coming with me, but I really wanted to hear how Emma was first. Such good news her condition hasn't deteriorated any further.'

By the time they reached the house, Sophie was ready by the door, bag packed, Lucy at her side. 'How is she?' they asked in unison.

'Her temperature's stable at least,' said Miss Walker with a smile. 'But Doctor Abbotts says she not out of the woods yet. Let's all keep our fingers crossed. Now, are you ready, Sophie?'

'May I go in and see her?' asked Sophie, trying to mask her urgency as she handed her coat to Mrs Howe. The hallway clock chimed once, announcing 10.30 a.m. Sophie's breath quickened. She was already half an hour late.

'You go on up, Miss Sophie,' said Mrs Howe. 'Don't wake her if she's sleeping, mind. After that, I'd suggest you have a lie-down to catch up on your sleep.'

'Of course.' Sophie bounded up the stairs and entered Emma's room. One of the tall shutters was folded back and the morning sun fell in a wide shaft onto her bed and the table beside it. Emma was fast asleep. Sophie glanced back to double check the door was closed, then went straight to the bedside drawer and pulled it open. Feeling at the back, she could only locate one tablet. She frowned, reaching around again, then crouched down to peer inside. The drawer rattled in its frame under the pressure of her hold.

'I've taken it,' whispered Emma, half opening her eyes and making Sophie start. '10 o'clock!' she added.

'*Phew!*' breathed Sophie, putting her hand to her chest.

Emma yawned. 'When's Stella coming?' Her eyes were fluttering, sleep already pulling her back.

'As soon as Doctor Abbotts says you can have visitors. I'll come back at 2 o'clock for your next tablet — if you're more awake we can talk properly.'

'Good idea,' whispered Emma. As she turned onto her back and closed her eyes, Sophie slid her hand to the back of the second drawer and retrieved the medicine box. She quickly extracted four more tablets and hid them in the back of the top drawer with the remaining one. It somehow felt safer to keep the daily dose separate from the box — that way if one or the other were found, they'd hopefully have at least *some* tablets left. She would remind Emma about where the box was later.

As Sophie closed the door behind her, Eliza appeared on the landing, carrying a bag of laundry. 'Miss Emma was helping herself to water when I popped in earlier.' She smiled reassuringly. 'That's a good sign if you ask me!'

Sophie nodded. 'It definitely is. I think she's going to get better.' Hearing her own words filled her with joy and relief.

A gentle tap on Sophie's door started her awake from where she'd been dozing on her bed. Eliza entered, carrying a tray with soup and sandwiches. Sophie yawned and sat up.

'Well, the good news is your sister's just had some soup and is asking for you.' Eliza set the tray down on the table by the window. 'Miss Walker tells us you didn't eat breakfast at Miss Lucy's this morning, so be sure to eat this all up.'

Sophie glanced at her carriage clock on the fireplace. It was almost 1.30 p.m.

'It smells delicious, Eliza!' she said, drawing a warm smile from the housemaid as she jumped off her bed. 'Please tell Emma I'll be there soon and not to fall asleep this time!'

When Sophie returned to visit Emma half an hour later, she was awake and sitting up in bed, watching Eliza adjust flowers in a vase on a side table. 'There, aren't they pretty now?' said Eliza, smiling and wiping her hands on her white apron. She quickly adjusted her mob cap, nodded, and left the room.

'They're from Lucy,' said Emma the moment the door closed. 'And *look!*' She picked up a small card from her bedside table and passed it to Sophie. The message read *Get well soon, dear Emms. Hope to see you very soon! Lucy (T&S!)*

Emma's cheeks, though still gaunt, were less flushed than earlier and her dark curls, newly brushed out, glistened in the sunlight. Apart from looking a little thinner, her sister was her old self for the first time in what felt like an age. Sophie cupped her hand over her mouth and giggled as she read the encrypted message from Stella and Tom. Then she remembered the medicine.

'Right,' she said after Emma had swallowed the tablet. 'That's four you've had. It's every 12 hours, so we'll have to start again at 2 o'clock in the morning, I'm afraid. It's a bit of a bore. But I'll wake you up. There are four more in the back of the drawer. The rest are in a box—'

'At the back of the second drawer!' said Emma, pointing. 'Don't worry, I checked earlier. I'm definitely feeling better. I was even hungry when I woke up and Mrs Howe said my temperature's dropped a bit.' She smiled and looked out towards the garden. 'I think it's starting to work!' She turned back to Sophie. 'Now *please*, tell me everything!'

Sophie recounted how she'd followed Lucy into the garden, crossed the lake and thought she'd been abandoned. Tears filled her eyes as she described battling with the boat and the laundry bag, then thinking about the clothes she'd found inside and Lucy talking about children from the future, and suddenly wondering if it could be true after all. 'I'm *so* glad I turned back.' She paused as her eyes fell to her lap. 'I... I'm sorry for being so beastly all the time. And for telling on you all that night Jack broke in last year. I *didn't know*—' As the words came tumbling out, it was as if an enormous weight were sliding off her shoulders.

'How *could* you know?' said Emma quickly. 'You hadn't seen the moles.' She reached to take her sister's hand. 'Besides, if you *hadn't* shouted the house awake, Mama and Papa wouldn't have come out — and Stella wouldn't have been there with her magic voice recording.' She frowned. 'Actually, that means Crawley might never have been caught for stealing!'

Sophie smiled at her little sister. It was so typical of her to see the best in everyone. And even though what she said made some sort of sense, Sophie knew it didn't excuse her terrible behaviour.

As the clock chimed three, Mrs Howe knocked and put her head around the door. 'Time for Miss Emma to rest, Miss Sophie. Two minutes.'

'When will I see Stella and Tom?' whispered Emma anxiously. 'They *mustn't* go back before I'm better.'

'Lucy's making a plan,' Sophie said in a lowered voice. 'Stella said the tablets take three days to start working properly, so hopefully after that. That means the day after tomorrow.' Sophie bit her lip. 'I don't know *how* Lucy's going to explain Stella and Tom, though! And I hope they don't get caught in her side room!'

'She'll think of something!' said Emma with a bright smile. 'She always does!'

* * *

Sophie kept her promise of coming in to wake Emma for her tablets at two in the morning, and then again at six before the household woke.

Nurse Bagshaw slept through the first visit and greeted Sophie with a smile for the second, using the opportunity once again to go to make tea. 'I think she's turned a corner,' she said with a smile as Sophie stood up to leave. 'Doctor's going to be pleasantly surprised later.'

In fact, it was mid-afternoon before Doctor Abbotts arrived, and in somewhat of a fluster. By this time Sophie had administered Emma two more tablets, completing her Day 2 dose. 'Twins!' he said, rolling his eyes to Mrs Howe as she opened the front door. 'That was a surprise, for *all* concerned.' He yawned as he handed his coat to Eliza and started following Mrs Howe up the stairs. 'Now, how is our young lady? I'm assuming you'd have sent a message if things had turned?'

Emma was sitting up in bed with Sophie and Miss Walker at her side when he entered the room. Mrs Howe handed him the note Nurse Bagshaw had left before retiring to sleep that morning, along with temperature readings Mrs Howe had taken in the few hours since. She also confirmed that Emma had started eating solid food.

'*Well,*' he said, as he removed his stethoscope from

her chest, 'that is quite a remarkable recovery! Your heart rate is perfect and your temperature's almost back to normal! Brava, young lady!'

'I feel *so* much better!' said Emma. '*And* I ate lunch! Can my friend Lucy visit me tomorrow? *Please!*' Doctor Abbotts shook his head and smiled.

'As far as I'm concerned, you are fine to receive visitors.' He glanced in turn at Mrs Howe and Miss Walker. 'Assuming no change tomorrow, I'd suggest we plan on getting her out the next day for some fresh air and a change of scene. All this sitting cooped up inside doesn't do anyone any good.' He winked at Emma. 'There's a whole world waiting for you outside!'

19
THE WAIT

The novelty and excitement of hiding in Lucy's room kept Stella, Tom and Lucy in good spirits over the first two days. Lucy, who was expert at creeping around the house at night, had managed to bring them food from the pantry — and keep guard when they needed to use the bathroom across the hall. She'd lent Stella a long, white nightdress with rosebud embroidery, and Tom a set of Arthur's striped pyjamas, which were far too long for him and brought about sniggered whispers as he stood in front of her armoire mirror.

After the drama of Sophie's night walk, Lucy had persuaded her mother that reading quietly alone was helping take her mind off Emma's predicament, so was able to spend longer than usual in her room alone after mealtimes. Nancy, the maid, and Mrs Dunford, the housekeeper, always knocked before coming in — which wasn't too often once the cleaning was done. Nevertheless, she kept a chair placed against the door just to be on the safe side.

Lucy couldn't help giggling at the look on Tom and Stella's face as they'd emerged from the luggage room the first morning — mouths open, eyes wide as they took in their surroundings. Having been in the same situation so recently in their time, she knew *exactly* how they were feeling. She proceeded to give them a guided tour of each item of furniture, what she kept in it, and who had given her the various ornaments that stood on her dresser and mantlepiece. Stella had marvelled at the array of dresses and coats in her armoire and the delicate embroidery on her undergarments. Tom, meanwhile, was far more interested in her fireplace, the family portrait above it, and a fountain pen and blotter set which she proudly showed off and let them practise with.

'Wow! This is *so cool* — like writing with blue blood!' Tom exclaimed.

After Sophie had moved back home on the first morning, Lucy had asked if she could send flowers to Emma and couldn't resist adding the coded message at the end of the note.

'What's *T&S*?' her governess, Miss Cowley, had asked with a puzzled frown as she stood over her.

Lucy had paused, her cheeks reddening as she put the card into the little envelope. Then she'd smiled. '*Trouble and strife!* That's what we call ourselves when we go for our garden walks. I thought it might cheer Emms up!'

It was when Miss Walker telephoned late on the second afternoon, with the news that Emma could receive visitors the next afternoon, if she remained stable, that the children put the next part of their plan into action.

Lucy insisted she would go across the gardens rather than be collected. To her annoyance, her mother had insisted Miss Cowley walk across with her, but even as she remonstrated, she realised it could still work.

That night, they went over everything one last time. 'Right,' said Lucy. 'Papa and Mama will be leaving for the country after we've been to the early Easter service. The servants all go to the main service, so the kitchen will be clear between ten and midday. I'll be in the library from half-past ten doing my French catch-up lesson with Miss Cowley.' She gave them a broad grin. 'I'll make an excuse to come up, so I can let you know the coast is clear. You know the rest. I can't *wait* to see the look on Emma's face!'

．　．　．

The visit was arranged for 3 o'clock. Ten minutes into her lesson, Lucy asked to be excused to use the lavatory. Stella and Tom were waiting, as planned, shoes in hand. None of Lucy's shoes had fitted Stella in the end, so they'd resorted to colouring her trainers with brown polish, which Lucy had borrowed from the boot room. 'They don't look exactly old-fashioned,' Tom had said with a frown when they'd finished.

'I know,' Lucy had replied with a shrug. 'We'll just have to *cross that bridge when we come to it* if anyone asks.' Then she'd furrowed her brow, realising there was a lot of *bridge crossing* going on in their planning right now.

Lucy led them quickly down the stairs and out through the kitchen, picking up two bread rolls as she passed. She unlocked the kitchen door and let them out. 'Here, take these. I'd better go. See you later!' As Stella and Tom bent to put on their shoes, she re-locked the door and sped back up to Miss Cowley in the library.

'Phew!' that's better, she said, retaking her seat. 'I was *bursting*!'

Stella checked the little watch that Lucy had lent her, and which was pinned to the front of her dress. They had nearly four hours to kill and had already planned to head to the lake. The sun was shining, and they now had time to practise their accents, and the muddled story they'd agreed with Lucy.

As they made their way across the lawn towards the lake path, a young girl with her nanny — or perhaps it was a governess — appeared on the far side of the gardens, coming in their direction. 'Just nod and smile. I'll do the rest,' Stella whispered. As they drew closer, she curled her mouth up. 'Good morning!' she said brightly as they passed. Tom nodded beside her.

'And a lovely one it is too,' said the lady, coming to a halt. 'I don't believe we've met, have we? I'm Miss Smythe and this is my charge, Elizabeth Howard.'

Stella put on another wide smile, then stopped and turned. 'How lovely to meet you,' she said in a slightly grander voice than she'd intended. Tom's smirk, disguised as a cough, made her cheeks flush. 'I'm Stella and this is my brother Tom. Actually, we're new to the gardens — we're *just* going to explore.' She smiled at the little girl, who must have been around the age of six, before continuing. '*Mama's* just unpack—' She blinked and stopped herself, realising that the idea of a mother doing any sort of unpacking would probably sound bonkers.

'Well, don't miss the lake down there. It's stunning at this time of year!' said Miss Smythe, pointing to the path. Unnoticed by her nanny, the little girl Elizabeth was suddenly staring at Stella's trainers with a twisted frown.

'Ooh! Look at that bird!' said Tom, pointing to a tree. The little girl cast her gaze upwards, searching left, then right, trying to follow his arm.

'The lake's *just* where we're going! *Thank* you!' said Stella, causing Tom to clear his throat again. 'Have a good morning. It was so lovely to meet you!'

'*Slick!*' said Tom, crossing his eyes as they continued in the direction of the lake. 'You should be an actress, Stell!'

His sister frowned, then sniggered, as she picked out the lake path. 'Yeah, think I might have overdone it!'

At five to three, and after much more practising of accents and back story at the Thinking Log, Tom and Stella left the lake and headed towards Emma's house. As her patio garden gate came into view, they saw Lucy with her governess in the distance, cutting across in the same direction.

'Here goes!' whispered Stella, then threw her arms into the air. 'Lucy!' she called. *'Lucy!'* Lucy, who had been in conversation with Miss Cowley, stopped and turned. Immediately, her face lit up and she began waving back.

'Stella!' she called, then said something to Miss Cowley before they both began walking hurriedly in their direction.

'When did you get back?' Lucy asked as they approached, her eyes dramatically wide.

'Yesterday,' said Stella, beaming. Tom stood at her side, nodding. Stella turned to Miss Cowley and smiled. 'How do you do?' she said. 'I'm Stella Hawken and this is my brother Tom.' She turned back to Lucy. '*Mama* told me Emma's been unwell. It sounds *terrible*. We were *just* going to ask how she is—'

'She's better — and that's *exactly* where we're going!' said Lucy. 'You *must* join us!'

'Lucy, dear, I'm not sure—'

'I'm sure it will be fine, Miss Cowley. Emma was only saying last week how much she's missed seeing Stella and Tom. And I'm sure Miss Walker will be delighted to see them!' As they had walked to meet Tom and Stella, Lucy had crossed her fingers and explained that they lived abroad but came each year to visit their mother's cousin, who lived on the far side of the gardens, and that they knew Sophie and Emma well.

Eliza, the housemaid, was in the Gladstone household kitchen setting up cups and saucers on a tray when

Lucy tapped on the back door. This was the normal routine she and Emma had for calling on each other when meeting for garden walks.

'Hello there, Miss Lucy,' said Eliza, glancing at Stella and Tom with a surprised smile. 'Miss Emma's been talking about your visit all morning.'

'Right on time!' declared Mrs Howe, appearing from the back stairs. Thank you for escorting her, Miss Cowley. She turned her gaze towards Tom and Stella. 'Now, *whom* have we here?'

'This is Stella and Tom,' said Lucy quickly. 'They've just moved back to Europe from Australia and are staying with their mama's cousin in the gardens. Emma met them last year, and I know she'd *love* to see them. May they visit with us?'

'How do you do?' said Stella, smiling sweetly. She gently pinched Tom from behind.

'Hello,' he said in an awkward voice. 'It's *great* to meet you!' he added quickly, then swallowed hard. The words were out before he could stop them, drawing a startled look from Mrs Howe.

'Pleased to meet you, Miss Stella and Master Tom.' She paused and gave a puzzled frown, as if trying to place them. 'Your names certainly ring a bell.' Then her mouth fell open. '*Of course!* That terrible business with Crawley and the silver — I gather you were quite the heroine,' she said, smiling at Stella.

'*Exactly,*' said Lucy.

'Well,' Mrs Howe went on, 'Miss Emma seems perfectly back to normal. A quite remarkable recovery, according to Doctor Abbotts. She was thrilled when he said she could get up this morning. And he did say that seeing friends again will do her good. Eliza, will you please set up extra cups and plates to bring up to the drawing room?'

'Of course, Mrs Howe.' Eliza, already back at the table and buttering scones, reached for more cups from a tall pine dresser that stood against the wall beside the range.

'In you come now. And leave your shoes in the boot room.' Mrs Howe's eyes flickered as they fell on Stella's trainers. She cleared her throat. 'Oh, and, er, thank you, Miss Cowley. I understand Miss Walker will accompany Lucy back.'

'*Actually,* I might walk with Stella and Tom,' said Lucy brightly.

As they passed through the hallway on their way to the first floor, Stella caught sight of herself in the elaborate gilt mirror that hung on the wall opposite the staircase. The night before, Lucy had helped her separate her white-blond waves of hair into strands, then twist and fasten them at the end. In the morning they had unravelled into ringlets, which Stella now admired as they fell around her shoulders onto the laced trim around the top of her dress. To make her look *even more authentic*, Lucy had tied one lock of Stella's hair with a blue ribbon on one side of her parting. Stella couldn't imagine ever wearing anything like this in her own time, but right now both her pale blue dress — with its frilly cuffs, neck lace and all — and the black woollen stockings she wore beneath it felt the most natural thing in the world.

She wished she could say the same for Tom's clothes. Lucy's brother Arthur was clearly taller and wider than him and, as with his first clothes fitting on the Island, it had taken some careful arranging that morning to disguise the mismatch. The rolled-over waist of his breeches, hidden below his brown corduroy jacket, at least ensured the trouser legs ended where they were meant to, just below his knee. However, they could do nothing about the wide shoulders and over-long jacket sleeves, and in the end had resorted to turning the cuffs under, hoping no one would notice when they occasionally unfurled. The shirt underneath was equally oversized, though hidden beneath the jacket and a small black tie. Thankfully, Arthur's knee-length socks and leather ankle boots fitted. They had all agreed a back-up story about lost luggage if anyone asked, but Lucy had said that was *highly unlikely*, as questioning someone's appearance would be impolite *unless it involved one of the servants.* This had led to startled glances from Stella and Tom.

Now, as they stood outside the door to what Stella supposed must be the drawing room, but which in their own house led to her parents' bedroom, her heart lifted. She'd never dreamt she'd meet Emma again so soon. But here they were — and she couldn't wait. At that moment, something Charlie Green had said about *staying strong* pricked at the back of her mind. But as Mrs Howe turned the gleaming brass door handle, the thought evaporated.

20

REUNITED

A s they entered, afternoon sunlight flooded through the drawing room, which ran from the road at the front of the house to the gardens at the back. An oval-shaped table, covered in a white tablecloth and laid out with a silver teapot, cups and saucers, cake stands, and a glass jug stood by the tall French windows that looked over the gardens.

Emma sat back on an elaborate, crimson-coloured sofa, one foot raised on a stool, the other on the rug beside Harry, who dozed in a basket. She wore a pale pink muslin dress, with neck lace similar to Stella's, and her legs and feet were bare. As the children appeared, her eyes widened, and she immediately sat forward and waved vigorously. Stella grinned broadly and waved back. Tom, beside her, did the same. In that moment, Stella could see that

Emma hadn't really changed, other than looking a little thinner in the face and possibly a little taller — though that was hard to tell until she stood up. Miss Walker, whom Stella instantly recognised sitting beside Sophie on the opposite sofa, had hardly changed either.

'Oh, *dearest* Emms, it's *so* good to see you up at last!' said Lucy, rushing over. 'And just *look* who I've brought to see you! Tom and Stella are here for a few days from *Europe* staying with their mama's cousin, like last year.' She raised her eyebrows and slipped Emma a knowing glance, then turned her attention to Miss Walker and Sophie. 'Isn't it *exciting?*'

A brief silence followed as everyone absorbed Lucy's introduction. Tom and Stella hovered just inside the doorway beside Mrs Howe. Then Emma clasped her hands. 'This is the *best* day — and what a *wonderful* surprise! Please come and sit!' Her hands fluttered, beckoning Stella and Tom over.

'Hi, Emma!' said Tom with a broad grin. 'How's Harry?' He bent down and started stroking the little white terrier's head. Stella sighed inwardly. They'd just spent half an hour at the lake practising *Hello* for introductions!

'Hello, Emma. I'm sorry to hear about your leg,' she said with a smile. 'Hello, Miss Walker. Hello, Sophie.'

'Hi, both,' Tom said, drawing another inward sigh from Stella.

'Stella and Tom, what a *lovely* surprise!' said Miss Walker, standing up. She turned to Mrs Howe. 'Don't worry, Mrs Howe, I'll pour the tea.'

'Well, if you're sure, Miss Walker. Eliza has plenty to be getting on with—'

'Of course!'

As Eliza and Mrs Howe left the room, and Emma exchanged excited whispers with Lucy, Stella, and Tom, Miss Walker headed towards the tea table. 'Now, what have you been up to since I saw you last, Tom and Stella? It was just before all that terrible business with Sid Crawley, as I recall?'

The children exchanged wild glances behind her back as she reached across the table for the silver teapot. Lucy mouthed something and nodded vigorously at Stella, who had momentarily frozen.

'*Travelling,*' Stella finally said, then her cheeks went numb as she forgot what she was supposed to say next.

'Her father was governor in Australia,' added Lucy, as Miss Walker started to pour the tea, 'and now they live in Paris and get to go all over Europe. They're only staying for a few days, aren't you, Stella?'

'That's right!' said Stella.

'You know, I had somehow recalled Emma saying you were *Lucy's* cousins,' said Miss Walker, turning her head briefly with a puzzled frown. She turned back and reached for the milk jug.

'Oh, that was my silly mistake,' said Emma, widening her eyes at the children around her. 'They're actually Lucy's *neighbour's* SECOND cousins. She doesn't have any children, so she enjoys having them to visit.'

'Does your *governess* go with you to Europe, Stella?' Lucy added quickly, clearly trying to steer the subject away from cousins. She nodded briskly at Stella and smiled.

'Oh, of course!' Stella replied, letting out a breath and marvelling at everyone's improvisation. 'We still have to do our *lessons!*'

'She's actually called Miss Smythe,' declared Tom with a satisfied grin.

'Well, how wonderfully exotic!' said Miss Walker, turning and holding up a cup of tea in one hand and a jug in the other. 'Now, who would like tea and who would prefer lemonade? And, please, come and help yourselves to sandwiches.'

Emma, who had been resting her leg *as her own precaution*, was able to get up and walk to the table. 'Let's sit here and enjoy the garden view,' she said. 'Doctor

Abbotts said I can go out tomorrow if I don't faint today — this will do nicely for now, though!'

Crustless smoked salmon finger sandwiches, home-made scones and what looked like oatmeal biscuits sat in delicate layers on three tabletop cake stands. Floral china plates, cups and saucers edged in dark blue and gold were set around the table, along with engraved glass tumblers, while cut-glass pots with silver tops, containing cream and jam, each with a silver teaspoon to one side, sat between the cake stands.

Soon they were all drinking and eating, with Stella occasionally pressing Tom's foot under the table to stop him from piling his plate up.

Unsurprisingly, the major topic of conversation was Emma's fall, how they'd thought the cut was healing, then how ill she'd suddenly become — and how the telegrams to Mr and Mrs Gladstone had failed to reach them when things looked serious. At this point in the conversation, Sophie had fallen silent and looked a little pale, which didn't go unnoticed by Stella, or Miss Walker. The conversation then turned to Emma's unexpected recovery, and confirmation that the latest telegram reporting that all was well had reached Mr and Mrs Gladstone's hotel that morning. Tom kept trying to pick his moment to ask about Jack, but each time he opened his mouth someone else jumped into the conversation.

'Doctor Abbotts said this morning he'd never seen things turn so quick—,' said Miss Walker.

The doorbell downstairs rang, interrupting her flow.

'Anyway,' she continued, 'by all accounts you've been very lucky, Emma.'

There was a knock at the door and the doctor entered, accompanied by Mrs Howe. 'Why, good afternoon, Doctor Abbotts — back so soon! This is a surprise! We were just talking about you.' Miss Walker stood up.

'Sit down, sit down, all!' he said, quickly gesturing to the children who had started to move from their seats. 'I was just passing on my way back from the twins, so thought I'd see how our patient is doing.' He glanced at the half-eaten scone on Emma's plate. 'Well,' he said, nodding, 'by the looks of things, *very* well indeed!' He turned to Mrs Howe, 'Temperature normal since I left this morning, you said?'

'It's been a good 36 hours now,' said Mrs Howe, nodding.

'Here,' said Emma, sticking out her leg for inspection. 'You can check it again if you like.' Doctor Abbotts crouched down for a closer look.

'Well, as I said earlier, this really is quite something,' he muttered.

'Can I still go out tomorrow?' said Emma as he let her leg down.

'I think getting out will do you a world of good, young lady!' He stood up and turned to Mrs Howe. 'Let's cancel tomorrow morning's visit, Mrs Howe. I don't think you'll be needing me. I'll send my invoice at the end of the week.' He turned and winked at the children. 'Fresh air, fun and friends — that's all you need now!'

The moment the doctor closed the door, Stella seized the moment. She knew just how desperate Tom was for news of Jack.

'How is Jack, by the way?' she said. 'We'd *love* to see him while we're here.' Tom smiled and nodded vigorously.

'So happy last time I saw him!' said Emma. She smiled with a look of pride. 'After all that horrid business last year, Papa helped his family move to a little house in Tooting — new ones made by the government or something.' She cocked her head to one side. '*Well*, it's actually three rooms on the ground floor, with a garden. Papa took me when they moved in.' She brushed back her dark ringlets and smiled. '*And* Jack goes to school most days *and* Papa helped Jacob find lots more work.' She sighed. 'They haven't been here for a little while, though. Jacob's been really busy — Papa told me they're saving to move to America. I think they might be going quite soon.'

'Wow!' said Tom. It had never occurred to him that people in this time could suddenly *decide* to move to America. Now that he had heard Jack might be moving, he wanted to see him more than ever. 'How will they get there? You can't exactly *fly*, can you?'

Miss Walker clunked her teacup onto her saucer and burst out laughing. 'You really are very funny, Tom. They'll get there exactly the same way you travelled from Australia!'

Tom stared at her blankly.

'By ship, of course, silly!' said Emma, giggling.

'Exactly,' said Miss Walker. 'Steam ships sail there every week. In fact,' she went on, 'the world's largest passenger ship is sailing to New York in three days. Most exciting. It's all over the news!'

'I wonder if it's the one Jack's going on?' said Emma.

Stella jerked forward in her seat. She darted a look at Tom, who clearly hadn't made the connection and was busy absorbing the story with interest.

'I thought the Titanic was just for rich families?' said Sophie with a frown.

'It is mostly,' said Miss Walker. 'But they have third class cabins at the bottom. All very crowded, but nice canteens to eat in by all accounts. Quite a treat for the working-class families emigrating, I'd say.'

The room seemed to have clouded over and the conversation floated in the air around Stella as her stomach began to churn.

'Are you all right, Stella?' she heard Miss Walker ask.

'Er, oh, I... I'm fine. I think I have a bit of indigestion.'

'Actually, I think Jack's family really *might* be on it!' Sophie said. 'The other day I heard Papa telling Mama about someone travelling to New York in style — deserving a new start or something.' She blushed, remembering how she'd been listening through the door, wondering if they'd been talking about her or Emma. She glanced around the table apologetically. 'I didn't hear the whole conversation though.'

Stella's stomach continued to turn. Could this be what Margaret's letter meant about 'water'? She had assumed it had been to do with taking the tablets.

She stole another glance at Tom, whose cheeks were now pale as he stared at the space in front of him, mouth down. He knew the ship's name, of course — thank goodness he hadn't said anything. She let out a low, shuddering breath, knowing there was nothing they could say to anyone. Then she breathed back in, her mind set. There was something they could do, however, and for that they needed to stay calm — and strong. In that moment, Charlie's words in the café made sense.

She was just trying to find a way to frame her question about visiting Jack when Sophie jumped up and turned to Miss Walker.

'Miss Walker. Let's forget Hyde Park and the Easter Fair. Can Stella, Tom, and Lucy join us on my belated birthday trip into town tomorrow? We could turn it into a surprise visit to Jack to say goodbye?' She then glanced sideways and smiled at the children around the table.

21
CROSSING BRIDGES

All eyes were on Miss Walker as Sophie's suggestion hung in the air.

'*Say yes. Say yes,*' Tom whispered to himself. His tummy felt empty and dark. He swallowed hard as he caught Stella's eye, determined not to let tears appear. Stella blinked once at him, signalling she understood.

'What a *super* idea!' Emma clapped her hands together, causing Harry to growl in his basket. She turned to Tom and Stella, eyes bright. 'It's Sophie's birthday treat — we're taking a taxicab!'

Miss Walker paused, as if doing mental arithmetic. 'Well,' she finally said, 'it'll be three on each seat, but I suppose we can *just* about fit. If your mamas and papas give their blessing, then why not?' She leaned forward and put her hand on Sophie's. 'Thank you, Sophie, for your suggestion.' She glanced down and flipped up the small watch that was pinned to her blouse. 'It's gone four. Time for you to get some rest, Emma. We'll leave at 11 tomorrow. Lucy, please ask Miss Cowley to escort you to the front by 10.45.' She glanced at Stella and Tom. 'Will your—'

'They can walk around with me!' cut in Lucy. Her skin tingled. With the whole outing a surprise, she had no idea how she would get Stella and Tom in and out of her house — they'd just have to *cross that bridge when they came to it.*

Lucy announced to Miss Walker that she didn't need accompanying back through the gardens. 'Besides,' she added with a smile, 'I have Stella and Tom with me, and they're used to being *independent.*' Miss Walker narrowed her eyes, clearly unconvinced by the logic of this reasoning. However, given the fine weather and the number of times Lucy and Emma had met alone in the gardens with their parents' blessing, Lucy felt sure she would agree. She was right.

'In that case, we look forward to seeing you all tomorrow,' said Miss Walker. 'The weather's set fair, so no need for coats.' She rang the bell to call Eliza to take them down.

'Thank you so much for tea,' Stella said as they left, and gently nudged Tom in the side.

'Thanks so much,' he said.

'It was *such* fun! Thank you,' added Lucy. 'See you tomorrow, Emms and Sophie!' The three children then followed Eliza down to the garden back door.

The moment Tom had heard the word *Titanic*, something changed inside of him. Suddenly, he felt much older and much wiser. And he knew that, for everyone's sake, he must bury the panic and desperation he was feeling and try to act normally. A moment's exchanged glances with Stella had told him she felt the same way.

'I can't wait to see Jack!' he said, trying to inject energy into his voice as they hurried across the lawn.

Lucy fixed her gaze on the grass in front of her as they marched. 'Now, we *just* need to make a plan to get you in and out of the house.' She looked up as the path to the lake came into view. 'Let's go to the Thinking Log while I work something out.'

The afternoon sun had dipped behind the trees by the time they arrived, and the early flowering buds on the Azalea bushes had closed. Even so, a magical calm hung over and around the lake.

As they took their seats and looked out across the water, what felt like a tiny electric shock seared through Stella. Would everything be okay back at home? They had been away three days now. What if time *hadn't* stood still? Her breathing quickened as she pictured her mother entering their bedrooms to find their beds empty. Then her stomach knotted. What if they didn't get to Jack in time? Would that steal away the future they knew? Or even *stop* the moles from coming back?

'Are you all right, Stella?' said Lucy, grasping her arm. Stella forced her mouth into a smile.

'I'm fine,' she said quickly. There was no way she wanted to set Tom panicking — for both their sakes she needed to stay calm and strong.

After a few minutes of Lucy studying her boots and muttering to herself, during which Tom and Stella stared across the lake in silence, Lucy jumped up. '*If you fail to plan*, etcetera,' she declared. 'It's a little complicated. But I *think* I have a plan!'

It was almost five by the time the children made their way back to the house. Nancy was in the kitchen rolling out pastry. A large pot bubbled on the range, filling the air with delicious aromas of lamb and onions.

'Come on in, Miss Lucy! How's Miss Emma? Did you have a pleasant visit?' Nancy wiped her hands on her long white apron. 'Hello there.' She raised her eyebrows and smiled at Stella and Tom.

At that moment, Mrs Dunford, the housekeeper,

appeared through the far door. 'There you are. Now, how is Miss Emma?'

'She's *fully* recovered!' said Lucy, beaming. She bent to remove her shoes, indicating to Tom and Stella that they should do the same. 'Mrs Dunford, Nancy,' she said as they all stood up, 'may I introduce Stella and Tom Hawken. They're friends of Emma's from abroad and are staying with their mama's cousin here in the gardens for a few days.'

'How do you do?' said Stella, smiling.

'Pleased to meet you,' added Tom, without requiring any nudge from Stella.

'We're going on a trip with Sophie and Emma tomorrow to *belatedly* celebrate Sophie's birthday,' said Lucy, 'but Stella and Tom's luggage hasn't arrived, so I've offered to lend them some clothes.' She tossed her head back and rolled her eyes. 'Emma's are too small, and Sophie's are too big — and there's nothing for Tom, of course!

'I know Mama won't mind,' she went on brightly. 'Remember the outfit she lent to Mrs Marlowe from the bakery when they had the meeting at Parliament last month?'

'I do indeed!' said Mrs Dunford. 'And quite a lady she looked too!' She glanced at Tom's outfit and narrowed her eyes — either, Lucy thought, because it rang a bell as being one of Arthur's, or because she could see it was the wrong size. But she didn't comment. Luckily, the popular style of the muslin day dress Lucy had lent Stella meant it didn't draw attention.

Lucy insisted they didn't need help with clothes selection and that there was no need to disturb Miss Cowley, who was reading in the library. Half an hour later, after choosing a different outfit for Tom and some sneaking around and peering through doorways, all of which made her skin tingle, she chose a moment when the kitchen was empty to retrieve Tom and Stella's shoes. A few minutes later, with Stella and Tom safely hidden back in the luggage room, she came back down and made a point of crossing paths with Mrs Dunford to confirm that her guests had just left through the back. She then sought out Miss Cowley in the library to update her on tomorrow's trip and let her know that Tom and Stella would call to walk round with them in the morning.

'We have to warn Jack!' said Tom the moment Lucy left the room. 'What are we going to do, Stell?' His eyes were wide and filled with fear.

'I know,' said Stella. *'I know.'* She paced up and

down inside the luggage room, trying to focus on Charlie's words telling her to *stay strong*. She'd been thinking through their options for the last ten minutes and not getting anywhere. If Jack's family were due to take the Titanic, they needed to get him alone and explain. But *how* could they do this without telling him about the event that would unfold?

'We *can't* tell him the truth, Tom. We just can't,' she said. 'No one would believe him if he tried to warn them. And if he knew but couldn't tell, he'd feel *so* guilty.' The weight of responsibility was unbearable.

'And anyway, what if we can't get him alone?' said Tom despairingly. He stared at his feet, deep in thought, then looked up. 'A NOTE!' he said. 'We don't have to say *why* — we can just warn him not to take the boat! He'll understand if it's from us!'

'Genius, Tom! *Genius!*' Despite feeling sick at the continued enormity of it all, Stella found herself smiling.

Later that evening, before Lucy went down to eat with Miss Cowley, Stella asked if they could borrow a pen and paper to write a farewell note for Jack, just in case he wasn't there when they visited.

'Of course!' Lucy said, then eagerly showed them one more time how her fountain pen worked and where the paper and envelopes were, in case they made a mistake.

Despite their nervousness about being caught, she insisted they use her writing desk while she was having dinner, as the servants all worked downstairs during mealtimes. Even so, Tom pushed two chairs against the door.

After much back-and-forth whispered discussion, Tom and Stella both agreed they must keep their message simple and untraceable, just in case it fell into the wrong hands.

They were sure Jack would understand the urgency once he read it, and that he was clever enough to create some sort of diversion that would stop his family, and anyone else he knew, getting on the boat.

They also agreed that leaving it for him to find would be a last resort. They had no way of knowing whether he'd told his father Jacob about the time tunnel.

And even if he had, if others were there when Jack opened the letter and word got around about the message, no one would believe him until it was too late. Jack would then get accused of having special powers. Didn't they lock people like that up in this time? Or hang them even? It didn't bear thinking about.

They had to hand the letter to him personally — and they had to warn him to open it alone.

Their final draft, which they put in an envelope marked 'J', read:

Don't go on Titanic! <u>Urgent.</u>

Repeat.

<u>DON'T GO ON BOAT!</u>

TS

22
THE OUTING

They were all up at sunrise and, after some sneaking around, Lucy managed to smuggle Stella and Tom out to the gardens with bread and cheese for breakfast — though not before a close shave with Nancy, which had required them all to hide in a broom cupboard for five minutes.

With their letter written, Tom and Stella had felt a weight lift from their shoulders and agreed that, for Jack's family's sake, they must now act as normally as possible rather than dwell on an event over which they had no control. No one would believe any warnings they might try to give. They at least had a chance to save one family, and that they had to be thankful for.

As planned, they returned and knocked at the kitchen back door just after 10.30 a.m. — dressed in a new set of clothes from Lucy, and ready for the outing.

Stella had checked and rechecked she had the envelope in her dress pocket, which was buttoned at the top, making the letter both safe and quick to access. In the circumstances, they couldn't have been any more prepared.

'Good morning, Miss Stella and Master Tom. And very smart you look too!' Nancy winked and gave them a wide smile, then took them up to Miss Cowley, who stood in the hallway with Lucy. To everyone's relief, Lord and Lady Cuthbertson were staying the night in the country, so their paths didn't cross with Tom and Stella's.

As they all stepped out onto the Cuthbertsons' front porch, Tom and Stella struggled to rein in their glances. Adjusting to past time in the gardens and inside two houses was one thing. Venturing into the world outside was quite another. The tree-lined crescent, which curved gently away in both directions, was, of course, entirely familiar — as were its grand houses in their variety of pastel shades. But there the similarity ended. It was as if they were on a film set. The trees, smaller and fewer than in their time, cowered below the facades of the houses rather than competing for height. The kerbs, normally crammed nose-to-end with parked cars and vans, were empty apart from occasional piles of straw and horse manure that had been swept to the roadside, its odour still lingering. And in place of their sleek anonymous streetlamps, ornately decorated gas lamps rose from the pavements.

Tom's eyes rested on what looked like a black carriage parked a few houses away. *'Awesome!'* he whispered. He couldn't see the horse at the front, but had spotted its legs in the gap between the wheels and the back of the driver's bowler hat as he sat waiting on high. 'Are we going in one of those?' he said eagerly, pointing. With their plan in place, it felt good to put last night's worries at a distance.

'Not exactly!' said Lucy with a side smile.

Stella, meanwhile, tried not to stare as two young men in three-piece tweed suits, both wearing flat straw hats, hurried past, deep in conversation, one taking out his pocket watch to check the time. On the opposite pavement, farther along, a lady wearing a white blouse with billowing sleeves and a blue ankle-length skirt held a child's hand as they ambled along, taking in the morning sunshine. Perched on top of her swept-up hair was an elaborate hat, decorated with feathers. Stella decided she preferred Miss Cowley's simpler straw boater with its white ribbon. Both the lady with the feather-filled hat and Miss Cowley wore white gloves, despite the warmth of the day.

Lucy and Stella were no exception when it came to

hats. The night before, Lucy had picked out one of her wide-brimmed *sailor hats*, as she called it, to lend Stella. In the end, they'd had to pin it towards the back of Stella's head, to stop it from falling off. Arthur's hats were far too big for Tom, so, to his relief, they had agreed he'd go without.

Stella was just marvelling at how the ladies' long swaying skirts didn't trip them up when the loud rumble of an approaching engine filled the air. A dark green car shaped like a rectangular box on tall narrow wheels roared past.

'Aren't these motorcars *loud*?' said Miss Cowley, smiling as she glanced sideways at Stella. 'Did you have one in Australia?'

Stella felt her face flush. 'Er... no, we didn't,' she replied uncertainly.

'They're perfectly safe,' said Lucy quickly, 'and *much* more comfortable than carriages, especially in winter! Anyway,' she added, 'we're going in a *taxicab* today. That means we get a private driver!'

Tom frowned, thinking how much more exciting it would be to go in a horse-drawn carriage.

As they rounded the corner, Miss Walker, Sophie and Emma emerged from their house and quickly spotted them and waved. At that moment, Tom felt a twinge telling him he needed a wee. He bit his lip, annoyed at himself for not using the loo after Stella before they left, then quietly gasped as he spotted the taxicab parked facing them at the foot of the steps. Perhaps going in one wouldn't be so boring after all! Its brass headlamps and maroon paintwork sparkled in the morning sun. As they drew closer, his eyes widened, taking in its wind-up handle on the front, like a toy car's, its white-rimmed wheels with gleaming spokes, and a tiny numberplate perched on top of the roof, as if ready to topple off at any moment.

'Good morning, all!' said Miss Walker as they came down the steps. 'It might be a bit of a squeeze, but the driver has said we should fit.' The driver, who wore a peaked cap, shirt and tie, and a long black jacket over dark trousers, smiled and nodded.

'*Perfect* timing!' said Emma, adjusting her blue sailor hat, which matched the colour of her dress.

'Good morning, everyone!' said Sophie, smiling behind her. She wore a pale peach muslin dress with lace on the shoulders and a white sailor hat, and carried a small velvet pouch. She darted a look at Miss Cowley, who was now chatting to Miss Walker, then held up three fingers and nodded, signalling that Emma had taken her first three tablets. She then pointed at her pouch and nodded. They had discussed at length that no matter how well Emma seemed, she must complete the seven-day course of tablets, and Stella was relieved to see this hadn't been forgotten in all the excitement. With the sudden distraction of Jack's fate, she was grateful more than ever for how much Sophie had risked to help them all.

'Have a good day, all!' said Miss Cowley. 'Stay together and do as Miss Walker asks!'

As the driver stepped forward to open the door, Tom pointed to behind the steering wheel at what looked like a miniature trumpet stuck to the glass partition. 'What's that?' he said.

Stella felt her cheeks turn red. 'Tom's never been in a *motor* taxicab before,' she said, glancing around.

'Oh, that's just the speaking tube,' said Emma, scrambling in as the driver held the door open. 'It means we can talk to the driver if we need to.' Tom followed her in. 'See, it comes through the other side here,' she said, nodding. She then plonked herself in the middle of the back seat and patted the spaces on either side. 'You two can come and sit here to get the view.'

Awesome! said Tom, drawing a sharp nudge from Stella as she climbed in behind him. Sophie and Lucy followed and sat opposite, putting their hands to their mouths to disguise their giggles.

'All right. We're all set. Picnic's in the front,' said Miss Walker, climbing in and sitting opposite Stella. The driver closed the door, climbed up ahead, and the engine roared into life.

'Tooting it is, Ma'am,' came his muffled voice through the tube. As they pulled away, a horse-drawn carriage with two top-hatted passengers passed them in the opposite direction, causing Tom's eyes to double in size.

The drive to Tooting took a good 45 minutes, during which Stella and Tom sat wide-eyed, taking in the view, and Tom tried to ignore his increasing twinges. Horse-drawn carriages, and open-top buses advertising SEEGER'S HAIR DYE, OMO, NESTLE MILK and more thronged the streets — all muddled in with more taxicabs; men, women, and children on bicycles; the occasional car and, on some streets, electric trams.

Amidst all of this, cloth-capped workers, young and old, wearing long white aprons, crisscrossed the streets hauling wooden carts carrying vegetables, fruit, flowers and a myriad other goods. Coal delivery carts regularly blocked the road, or stopped and turned across their path, their carthorses' heads tossing up and down. Meanwhile, men and women in an array of hats, caps, straw boaters and feathered hats periodically picked their way through the traffic on foot.

'Almost there,' said the taxi driver through the speaking tube. On either side of the street, wide awnings stretched out from shopfronts over the pavements.

'This is Tooting Broadway, so it's not far,' said Emma. 'I recognise it from when I came here with Papa last year.'

The traffic had become heavier again and the car slowed. Finally, they turned up a side street and, after a few more turns, into a narrower street with low-rise terraced houses with small front gardens behind picket fences.

'This is Jack's road!' said Emma, glancing at the passing doorways, trying to pick out the house numbers.

'It's a pretty street,' said Stella. 'I thought Jack would live somewhere more, er, well,' she hesitated, glancing around, '*crowded?*'

'Like Oliver Twist!' said Tom, nodding.

'Actually, they're new *worker cottages*,' said Emma. 'Jack's family were in a terrible slum before. Papa helped them with the council papers. It's only three rooms and a kitchen with a sink-bath, but they have a little garden at the back.' She rolled her eyes. 'Papa wouldn't let me go in. He said it could be *embarrassing*. But Jack told me they were really happy.'

'That's *so cool*—' Tom stopped mid-flow and glanced around awkwardly. 'That's so *kind* of your father,' he said. He shifted on his seat, trying to ignore the twinge that had grown much stronger in the last few minutes. Try as he might, he couldn't remember how to ask to go to the toilet.

'We're here! Number 53,' said Emma. The taxi was already slowing down and edging towards the pavement.

'Well, Miss Emma, an' ain't this a lovely surprise!' The lady who answered the door wore a large apron over her dress and had her sleeves rolled up. Her cheeks were flushed as she bounced a friendly smile between Emma, Stella and Tom, who had been nominated to knock while the others waited in the taxi.

'Hello, Betty. I hope you're well. May I introduce Stella and Tom. They're my friends who helped Jack when we had all that trouble last year. Is he here?'

'Well, I'll be darned. *Delighted* ter meet you! My Jack didn't stop talking about you all last summer — an' young Emma 'ere, of course. I'm afraid Jack's not' ere, loves. I expect you've come to say goodbye, 'ave you?'

Stella let out a silent sigh and felt for the envelope through her pocket.

'Are you really moving to America?' said Emma, eyes wide. 'How *exciting!*'

'Oh, no, not me, love — well, not for now at least! Sick as a dog I get, the minute I *sees* the sea!' At this

Betty let out a huge belly laugh. 'Just Jacob an' Jack goin' for now. I's stayin' 'ere wi' young Sidney an' we'll see 'ow they get on. If they make a go o' it, we'll join 'em. If not, they'll be back soon enough. *Three months* it's taken to save up them fares! This time tomorrow they'll be off to Southampton — next mornin' they'll be sailin' on the maiden voyage!'

She paused and narrowed her eyes at Tom, who was suddenly jigging from side to side. 'You need to use our privy, Tom?' she said with a smile.

'Oh, yes, please!' he replied. He was bursting and the sudden possibility of being able to go made holding it in even harder.

'Yer's most welcome, young man.' Betty stood to one side, pointing down the hall. 'It won't be as posh as wot yer used to, I's afraid, but don't tell me it ain't spotless! Straight out the back, through the scullery. Paper's 'anging on the back o' the door if you need it.'

Emma tilted her head to one side. 'I didn't realise Jack had a brother!'

'Oh, Sidney 'ain't no bruvver, love. We took him in at Christmas after 'e lost 'is family to the fever. Jacob didn't want to see him in the workhouse. E's as good as family now — on'y six 'e is, an' a sweet little thing, too. We're jus' sorting out the paperwork to adopt.'

'But how will you manage when they've gone?' said Emma.

'Oh, don't you go worryin' about me, Miss Emma. I've plenty o' laundry — an' sewing work besides — thanks to Jacob's customers. An' we have your pa to thank for them.' She put her hands on her hips and nodded. 'An' we'll take in a lodger or two. Six months we'll give it.'

Tom appeared back down the hallway, looking relieved at having used the toilet but clearly flustered as he tried to adjust and tuck in his oversized trousers.

'Thank you, Betty,' he said, blowing his cheeks out as he reappeared, then gave Stella a wide-eyed glance that suggested the 'privy' had been an 'interesting' experience.

'My pleasure, Tom,' Betty replied.

'When will Jack be back?' said Stella suddenly. She'd been trying to stay calm, but butterflies were now stirring in her tummy.

'Not for an hour or two, I don't expect. He's taken Sidney up the common to go rinkin'.' Betty nodded and peered beyond them. 'It'll only take a few minutes in one o' them posh taxicabs. Up just inside the entrance you'll find 'em — there's usually a crowd all roller skatin' around showing off. Provided the peelers don't come and break 'em up, that is.' She frowned and shook her head.

Stella released her grasp on the letter, her nerves settling.

'Why would the police prevent them *roller skating?*' said Emma. She knitted her eyebrows and wrinkled her nose.

'New by-laws, love. Tryin' to stop our young uns 'aving fun. An' a right pity it is too — fresh air, good exercise an' free it is, 'an they want to take it away from 'em! Now, if you tell your taxi driver Tooting Bec Common main entrance 'e'll 'ave you there in no time. I reckon you'll find 'em still there.'

'Perfect!' said Emma. 'We have a picnic with us — we're hoping they might join us!'

'I's sure they'd love that!' said Betty. 'Oh,' she added as they turned to leave. 'Please send my regards to your father, Miss Emma. Off you go now.'

As they turned to leave, Stella slowed her pace as she felt for the note once more. Should she leave it after all, just in case Jack wasn't there?

'Hurry, Stella!' Emma was beckoning from inside the car. 'We don't want to miss him!' The engine started. It was too late.

23

IN SEARCH OF JACK

As they pulled away, and as Betty waved from the gate, Stella darted a glance at Tom, who looked pale and anxious as he stared out of the car window. She had thought he was grimacing about the privy just now, but maybe he was trying to signal she should hand over the letter after all, to be on the safe side. Her stomach turned. She might have just blown their one chance of being sure Jack would get the message. Having told herself she would stay calm and focused, she felt panic setting in. But then again, Betty had said Jack would be there, hadn't she?

As their car pulled up, Stella's eyes roamed the crowds coming and going and gathered at the park entrance, desperately trying to pick out Jack's face. 'He's not there,' she whispered, her hopes dropping.

'There he is!' shouted Lucy, pointing. About 30 metres away, by some metal railings to the side of the main entrance, Jack was crouched down, helping a young boy adjust his roller skates.

'That must be Sidney!' said Emma. 'Poor boy. Betty said he's an orphan.'

Stella breathed out, feeling the tension fall away as she caught sight of Jack. She glanced at Tom. Despite his smile, his eyes looked anxious — and a little sad. Their time with Jack would be all too short, and she knew this would be playing on his mind.

'Do we have enough in our picnic for Jack *and* Sidney?' said Emma.

Miss Walker chuckled. 'Knowing Mrs Howe and Eliza, I'm sure we've more than enough!'

The driver alighted from the car and came round to open their door. Miss Walker immediately stepped round to organise the picnic hamper.

'Jack!' called Emma, already waving. *'Jack!'* Two older boys on roller skates whizzed past them, almost knocking into Sophie, and zipped into the park. Beyond the entrance Stella could see more children on skates, trying out different moves and having mini races as Easter strollers passed them by, most looking on with smiles.

Jack didn't recognise Emma at first, but as they

drew closer his eyebrows shot up and he grinned and bent down to say something to the little boy standing next to him. Then, as he stood back up, and as his gaze fell on first Stella, then Tom, his mouth opened. He froze for a moment, then narrowed his eyes, as if trying to focus. 'Is *tha'*—?'

'Yes!' called Emma, nodding vigorously. They were now within five metres.

'Well, *I'll be*—' His mouth froze open again.

Stella giggled, realising this was the first time she'd seen Jack lost for words. She glanced at Tom, who seemed to be holding back tears.

'They're visiting from *Europe!*' said Lucy as they finally approached. As she said the word *Europe*, she widened her eyes and cocked her head deliberately to one side, clearly hoping he'd understand the signal. Jack nodded slowly, then grinned and winked at Tom, then Stella.

'Well, this *is* a surprise. Ow grand ter see yer after all them *travels!*'

'Hello, Jack!' said Stella with a wide grin as she felt for the note in her pocket.

'Hi, Jack,' said Tom slightly awkwardly, but smiling all the same.

'Can you believe it?' added Emma, curling a finger around one of her dark curls. She then darted a look at Jack's companion. 'Oh, hello, you must be Sidney. I'm

Emma — and this is Lucy, Tom and Stella.' She looked back. Sophie and Miss Walker were retrieving the picnic basket from the taxi driver. 'Oh, and that's my sister Sophie and our governess, Miss Walker. We have a picnic, Jack. Please say you'll both join us!'

Jack's brown eyes beamed at them all from beneath his cloth cap. 'Well, what yer say, Sid? You got room for some picnic, eh?' He ruffled little Sidney's hair and winked at his audience. Sid's blue eyes widened under his mop of blonde hair as he fixed his stare on the picnic basket being carried in their direction by Miss Walker. Sophie, beside her, carried a tablecloth draped over her arm.

'Stella and Tom are leaving tomorrow,' said Lucy, 'so we came on an adventure to find you. And *now* we hear you're going to America on the *Titanic!* How terribly exciting!'

'Hello, Jack,' said Miss Walker as she and Sophie arrived.

'Top o' the mornin' to you, Miss Walker!' he said, smiling and removing his cap. He then put one roller skate forward and gave a theatrical bow, sweeping his cap in front of him, which made everyone laugh. 'An' same to you, Miss Sophie!' he said, and repeated the gesture all over again. By the time he stood up, little Sidney was doubled over in shrieks of laughter. Jack winked at his audience. 'Makin' Sidney smile, makes me smile! E's been through enough, 'e 'as.' He then ruffled Sidney's hair again.

Jack led them into the park a little way and found a spot just away from the paths. He and Sidney had to half clomp on the grass in their skates. The silly expressions they exchanged as they did so were clearly part of a ritual and made everyone else giggle again.

Stella smiled inwardly. Jack was as big-hearted as ever, and clearly went out of his way to keep Sidney in good spirits. How lucky Sid was to have been taken in by his family. She'd learned about the workhouses at school, and remembered Jack describing how they separated children from their parents, and forced them to scrub floors, or flogged them and locked them in coal cellars if they misbehaved — or sometimes just because the master was in a bad mood. Jack had never been in one himself but knew lots of street children who had. *''Ell on earth*, that's what we call it,' he had said with a glum face.

'This 'ere is posh linen!' said Jack as they all helped Miss Walker spread out the tablecloth. 'See this, Sidney? One day we'll afford this, you jus' wait!'

Miss Walker unpacked the picnic spread and they

were soon all enjoying sandwiches, scones, jam tarts and fruit — all washed down with lemonade.

'So when do you actually *sail?*' said Lucy. She held a half-eaten sandwich under her chin and cupped her other hand beneath it to catch the crumbs.

'Day after termorrow, 12 o'clock,' said Jack, smiling as he leaned forward and picked two jam tartlets from one of the plates. He passed one to Sidney, who popped it in his mouth and began chewing enthusiastically, clearly oblivious to any crumb catching etiquette. 'First stop France, then Ireland — then she's out across the Atlantic! Five days it'll take to get across.'

'Papa said the Titanic holds over 3,000 people,' said Sophie. 'And it has a gymnasium, squash courts and a swimming pool, not to mention the dining rooms and everything else! Imagine doing all that while you're *on water!*'

Jack laughed. 'Them's just fer the posh people, that 'is! Our cabins are *steerage* — right down the bottom — we don't get on deck or nothin'. Anyways, as Pa says, next time we see daylight it'll be in America — an' it don' get more excitin' than that!' He glanced at Sidney who, having finished his jam tart, had twisted round to look at the skaters on the path behind them.

'Can I 'ave a go, Jack?' he asked.

'You go on.' Jack winked at them all as Sidney

struggled to his feet and pulled his cap on. 'Stay where we can see yer, mind!'

'Course I will.' As Sidney started clomping towards the path, he turned and pulled one of their funny faces, making Jack roar with laughter. Stella felt for the note in her pocket again. She was desperate to catch Jack's eye, but so far it was proving impossible. Tom, meanwhile, kept widening his eyes at her.

'What work will you do when you get to America?' asked Miss Walker. A cloud passed over, casting her face into shade beneath her straw boater.

Jack squinted as the sun came back out from behind the cloud. 'Buildin' work mostly. Pa says there's plenty in the big cities, an' 'specially New York. 'E reckons 'e can earn enough to save for our own 'ouse one day. Fancy that, eh?' He looked round to check on Sidney, who was now roller skating slowly up and down the pathway behind.

'He's doing fine,' said Sophie with a smile. 'I've been watching him.'

'As 'andy a stone mason as they come, is Pa,' Jack went on. 'Not too bad at carpentry, neither.' He grinned at his audience, then reached for another jam tart. 'I'll 'elp him where 'e needs me, a course. An' I might find gardenin' work, if they'll 'ave me.' He winked and looked at the children in turn. 'Been readin' up on gardens, I 'ave. Wouldn't mind workin' in a big posh one like yours one day!' He laughed, looking all around, and just as his gaze landed on Sophie her eyes jumped wide.

'Look out!' she shouted, jumping up and peering beyond him. A woman's shriek followed, and they all turned to see Sidney and an elderly woman lying on the pathway.

Within seconds, Jack was on his feet and loping across the grass on his skates. The rest of the group followed, abandoning their half-eaten picnic. Other skaters and strollers stopped and gathered. A bowler-hatted gentleman was already stooping to help the lady. Meanwhile, the two older boys who'd almost skated into Sophie earlier had appeared and were pointing at Sidney, where he lay winded on his back.

'Yer shouldn't be out 'ere if you can't control yerself!' one of them yelled.

'Too right, yer clumsy oaf,' snarled the other.

By the time the children and Miss Walker arrived, a crowd had gathered, several muttering and pointing at Sidney who, with Jack's help, was now sitting up, his face white and still as marble. Only his blue eyes moved as he took in the scene around him. 'S'only shock,' said Jack. 'Yer'll be all right, Sid.'

A woman near the front of the crowd gasped as trickles of blood began fanning out across the old lady's forehead. The flow clearly had no intention of easing, and the white handkerchief with which the bowler-hatted man began furiously dabbing her was quickly turning bright red.

Stella felt a push from behind as more arrivals pressed in to see what had happened. 'Sorry, Miss,' someone said behind her, pushing her into Sophie, who stood in front of her. 'Mind yerselves back there!' The jostling and pushing carried on for a good 20 seconds before someone said to make way for a policeman. To Stella's relief, the pressure eased, and people stood back.

'*Why* do you need to push!' Stella turned to see Emma, who stood behind her between Miss Walker and Lucy, looking at a boy not much older than she was.

'Wasn't me!' he said with a scowl, and moved away.

'Here, Stella!' said Miss Walker, holding out her cotton picnic napkin. 'Pass this along, will you? Where's Tom, by the way?' She tried to peer through the heads.

Stella turned back in panic, then let out a silent breath as she spotted Tom sitting beside Sid, helping Jack comfort him.

'He's all right — he's over there with Jack,' said Sophie.

By the time the constable came through and reached the old lady, the blood flow had stemmed. 'I'm all right. I'm all right.' she muttered, more in frustration than pain as she tried to right her bird's nest hat. 'I just need to sit a moment more.'

'Disgraceful,' someone said from the crowd. 'That young child could have killed her.'

The policeman looked around to where Jack and Tom were now helping Sidney to his feet. The colour in his cheeks had returned, but his eyes filled with terror as he met the policeman's glare. 'It weren't me!' he said, his voice trembling.

'Yer it was! Them boys saw it,' someone shouted from the back of the crowd.

Jack's face tightened as he looked at the policeman. 'Constable, if 'e says it weren't 'im, it weren't 'im. E's an honest boy as yer'll find.'

'He's right. It wasn't him!' said Sophie.

'Where's your ma, boy?' said the policeman, ignoring Jack and Sophie.

'E's wi' me,' said Jack.

'E ain't got one,' someone shouted. 'E's an orphan — I reckon 'e escaped from the workhouse!'

'That ain't true.' Jack glanced around. 'E's part o' my family—'

Sidney's cheeks had turned white again and his feet rollered back and forth beneath his trembling knees. 'I AIN'T GOING TO NO WORKHOUSE!' he shouted, then yanked his arm free of Jack and skated off down the path into the common.

'Come back, Sid!' shouted Jack, as he and Tom gave chase.

'STOP THAT BOY!' bellowed the policeman. Then he reached for his whistle, took a breath so deep that it expanded his already ballooning stomach to bursting point, and blew until he was red in the face.

24
AN UNFORESEEN EXPENSE

'T OM!' yelled Stella, as she and Sophie pushed forward to try to follow, but the policeman blocked their path.

'Thank you, Constable,' said Miss Walker. 'Sophie and Stella, you're to stay right here.' Her tone was clipped and anxious as she reached forward and grasped Sophie by the arm. Around them, a crowd had regathered and was busy repeating the story of the young boy who had smacked into the old lady.

'But *Miss Walker*—' started Sophie.

'Them boys with you, are they?' interrupted the policeman, lifting an eyebrow.

'Yes,' said Sophie, 'And I can tell you—'

'Ah — 'ere they come!' he said, peering into the distance above her. He took out a pocket watch and nodded. 'Three minutes — a new record! Now, yer'll all need to stand back.'

The lady who had been knocked down was now up, supported by the man who'd been helping. 'Constable—'

'One moment, Ma'am.' A satisfied smile widened across his face as the boys came into closer view.

'What a *ghastly* man!' whispered Sophie.

Stella blinked back tears as two men approached, clutching Sidney by his collar and pulling him along on his skates. Jack and Tom were alongside, gesticulating and remonstrating. Then Jack skated ahead for the last few metres. 'Like I told, yer, Constable, it weren't 'im!'

'Pl... Pl... Please don't send me t... t... ter the w... w... workhouse!' Sidney hiccupped between sobs as they came to a halt in front of the policeman. Tears streaked his cheeks, and his eyes were red rimmed from crying.

'We 'elped stop 'im. You ask these men 'ere!' said Jack, glancing at the two men who still held Sidney's collar. They each tipped a nod at the policeman, whose eyes flickered with disappointment.

'Yes, but them boys saw 'im knock 'er over!' shouted someone from the crowd.

The gloating smile on the policeman's face returned. He shook his head at Jack. 'I've 'eard it all before, lad!' He cleared his throat and looked around uncertainly. 'An' there's enough witnesses 'ere as said it was this nipper!'

'They are *wrong*, Constable!' Sophie pulled away from Miss Walker's grip and pushed her way forward. 'I saw *exactly* what happened. It was those two older boys who accused him. They were skating far too fast and one went into Sidney and sent him flying into the unfortunate lady.' She glanced around. 'Where are they, anyway? They nearly knocked *me* over when we arrived here.'

'Thank goodness!' came a booming voice. The lady who'd been knocked over stood arm in arm with the gentleman who'd picked her up. It was now clear that he was her husband. 'If you'd let me get a word in edgeways, Constable, I could have told you it *wasn't* this young lad at all. As this young lady rightly said, it was those older ruffians who were the cause. And they have long gone, thanks to you! My cut is minor and I do not wish to bring charges, so will you please let these children go on their way. Come along now, Henry!' She looked the policeman up and down once, then turned with her husband and walked off.

'She's right,' someone said in the crowd. More people began nodding.

'Them older ruffians it was,' someone said.

'That's what I thought too,' said someone else. 'Poor young orphan bein' accused!'

The sun had gone in and a breeze was picking up and the crowd, sensing the drama was over, dispersed, leaving the picnic group, the minders and the policeman.

'Right!' said the policeman, narrowing his eyes. 'In that case, this young'un's lucky to get off with just a fine!'

Miss Walker let out a gasp.

'Yer *wot?*' said Jack, eyes wide.

'Don't you *yer wot* me, lad! There's by-laws against roller skatin' on public paths around 'ere. An' the by-law's the, er...' He paused and frowned. '...the, er, by-law. If this young lad's wi' you, you'll *both* need ter come along with me so we can take your *perticulers* an' arrange payment by yer family.'

Fresh tears flooded Sidney's eyes as he looked from the policeman to Jack and back again in bewilderment.

'What's a *by-law?*' Tom blurted out. He didn't like this bully policeman one little bit.

'Constable,' said Miss Walker, stepping forward. Her voice was shaking. 'Are you *really* going to fine this poor young child for getting exercise and fresh air? Look around you — there are any number of other children doing exactly the same thing! Hasn't he been through *enough?* Besides, everyone knows those rules are unfair — they don't even apply in most of London.'

'Unfair or not, *rules is rules,* Ma'am,' said the

policeman with a smug grin. He hooked his thumbs over the belt that surrounded his enormous stomach. '*Now,* let's not rack up any more fines, shall we? Like *wasting a policeman's time*—'

At that moment, Sophie stepped forward. 'I'll pay the fine,' she said, in a voice much older than her years. She reached inside the top of her dress and pulled out her velvet pouch.

'*Sophie!* You can't—'

'It's all right, Miss Walker. Mama told me to put it to good use and I shall.' She opened the pouch and took out two half-crown coins. 'Will this do?' she said.

The policeman's eyes expanded, and he flicked a glance at the two men still holding Sidney. 'Miss, to suggest that I can be *bribed*—' he said, fixing his eyes back on the coins.

'Oh, I'm definitely *not* trying to bribe you,' said Sophie with a sweet smile. 'I'd just like to pay Sidney's fine and I'm suggesting we *save everyone time* by you taking the payment and recording it when you get to the police station. I'm sure I've heard it can be done this way sometimes?' She smiled sweetly again, knowing full well that this was most definitely *not* how things worked.

The policeman glanced sideways at his helpers once more, then tipped back and forth on his feet, contemplating the clouds that had started to drift across the sky. 'Well,' he finally said, clearing his throat, 'I must say, this is highly *irregeller* and we do usually need to go to the police station. But in the *cerrcumstances* I may be able to consider makin' an *exception.*'

'Perfect!' said Sophie, and pushed the coins into his hand. The men who'd had Sidney by the collar released their grip and exchanged raised eyebrows with the constable.

'Come along now, Sidney and Jack,' said Miss Walker, reaching forward to take Sidney's hand. She gave the policeman a pencil thin smile and turned her back on him. 'Good day, Constable.'

'Oh, my goodness, you were brilliant, Sophie!' said Stella as they marched back to the picnic rug.

'Hear, hear!' said Emma, borrowing one of her papa's favourite phrases.

Miss Walker had folded the rug over the food that was left. As they pulled it back to reveal the remaining few sandwiches and jam tarts, Sidney's eyes lit up.

Jack nudged Sidney as they all sat down. 'What d'yer say to Miss Sophie, eh Sid? She sure 'as saved our bacon — even though you did nuffin' wrong.'

'Thank you very much, Miss,' Sidney whispered shyly to Sophie, then reached and took two jam tarts, making everyone giggle.

'Sure was kind o' you to give away your coins,' said Jack. 'We'll make it up to yer one day, soon as we can afford it.'

Sophie smiled. 'You're very welcome, Jack.' She lowered her eyes and picked at the hem of her dress. 'And don't ever *think* about paying me back. I'm really sorry for when I shouted the house awake last year. I had *no idea* about the time tu—'

Lucy coughed and nudged her, then made an announcement. 'Anyway, I've memorised the policeman's number so we can report him if we really want to! I think I'd like to be a *detective* when I'm older.'

Miss Walker leaned forward towards Sophie. 'You know, I'm extremely proud of you, Sophie. And I'm sure your mama and papa will be too.'

'Hear! Hear!' said Emma again.

The distress of the last ten minutes had given Stella a brief distraction from her worries about getting the note to Jack. But now the butterflies had returned — time was running out. She tried to catch Tom's eye, but he was ignoring her now, and staring anxiously at Jack.

From nowhere, spots of rain began to fall. They all looked up to see dark clouds approaching. 'We'd better get going before we all get soaked,' said Miss Walker, scrambling up. 'Will you and Sidney be all right, Jack?'

'Course! We'll be back in no time. Down'ill all the way it is from 'ere!'

As they all got to their feet and started helping clear the picnic leftovers, Stella darted a look at Jack. Finally, here was her chance. She would slip him the note and whisper her message.

She quickly reached to her pocket — her stomach turned. The button was open. She felt around inside, panic overwhelming her. The note was gone. She looked left and right on the ground, and out towards the path they'd come from. The rain was suddenly falling in grey diagonal lines and the taxi driver was striding towards them as everyone threw plates and leftovers into the basket. Tears filled her eyes. And now, as she remembered the crowds pressing against her and the young boys' voices in her ear, her cheeks burned. *How* could she have not realised?

'We better go, Sid!' said Jack, laughing.

'Bye, Stella and Tom! Was good to see yers — safe travels!'

'Bye, Jack, have a wonderful trip! Write to us and let us know how it is!'

'Hope to see you again!'

The farewell calls echoed around Stella as a mixture of tears and slanting rain blurred her vision. And there were Jack and Sidney loping across the grass towards the path, waving their hands in the air behind them.

25
LEAVING JACK

'My goodness, what a day!' exclaimed Miss Walker as the driver started the engine and they pulled away. The rain was coming down in sheets. 'I do hope the boys get back all right.'

'They'll be fine!' said Emma. 'I bet they've been roller skating in the rain before!'

'I've said it once, and I'll say it again. It was most kind of you, Sophie, to do that for Sidney,' said Miss Walker. 'I really can't wait to tell your mama and papa.'

'I didn't know you could pay fines to policemen,' said Emma.

'You can't!' said Sophie. 'But Papa told me some people do it to get off. It's called a *bribe*. And they call the police officers who take money like that *bent coppers!*'

Everyone apart from Stella and Tom burst into laughter, though Tom managed a smile.

'How did you know *he* was a bent copper?' said Lucy. She frowned at having missed a detective trick.

'I didn't,' said Sophie. Then she blushed. 'But it was worth the risk.'

'Are you all right, Stella?' asked Miss Walker.

Stella forced a smile. 'I'm fine,' she lied. 'Just a little tired.'

'Well, that's hardly a surprise with all your recent *travelling,*' said Emma, curling her finger around her hair. She slipped her arm through Stella's, causing tears to push behind Stella's eyes. Of course, Stella wasn't fine. She wasn't fine at all. She had messed up her chance to warn Jack not once, but twice. What this meant not only for Jack, but also for their future and the time tunnel, she had no idea. She darted a look at Tom, who was blinking fearfully at her. She felt sick and lightheaded. The scene before her began to sway, and she closed her eyes.

It was the silence that awoke her as the car engine switched off. Voices around her that had been part of her dream just now were suddenly loud and clear. Moments earlier, they had all been climbing up through the time tunnel, Jack and Sidney still in their skates and Miss Walker following with the picnic basket. As the door clunked open, she started fully awake, glancing all around. Then she remembered, and a wave of nausea hit her.

'Thank you *so* much for taking us,' said Lucy to Miss Walker. They all stood on the pavement outside Lucy's house. Nancy, the housemaid, stood at the top of the steps with the door open. The rain had cleared, and the late afternoon sky was bright again.

'Thank you so much,' said Stella. She forced her mouth into a smile, willing the tears not to come.

Miss Walker put her hand to her straw boater as a breeze passed through. 'Well, I'm glad you caught up on some sleep! When are you going back to Europe?'

'Early tomorrow,' said Tom quickly. He then flashed a determined glance at Stella.

'Oh, I do wish you could stay longer!' said Emma. She stepped forward to hug Stella. 'And thank you for both coming to see me when I was ill. You've made me feel *so much* better!' She stepped back, smiled, and cocked her head to one side. 'We must *definitely* meet up again next time!'

Stella returned her broad smile, but didn't dare speak for fear of breaking down.

'Of course!' said Tom.

'Well,' said Lucy, slipping a sideways glance at Miss Walker, who had stepped away to talk with Nancy, 'as Mama says, *time flies.* I don't suppose it will feel *that* long before we *all* see each other again.'

Stella was desperate to say something about Jack. Anything that might stop him from taking the ship. But the words wouldn't come, and in that moment she realised she had to let go. Events were larger than them all, and nothing she could say would change them. Besides, it was too enormous a burden to pass on, and even if Lucy, Emma and Sophie believed her, no one else would. She stepped forward and hugged Sophie. 'It was lovely to meet you properly this time,' she said. 'I *hope* we'll see you again.' A lump rose in her throat.

'Me too,' said Sophie, then whispered, *'We'll finish Emma's tablets. She had today's last one after the picnic,'* making Stella want to cry all over again.

'Come along in now,' said Miss Cowley, who had appeared at the top of the steps.

'Thank you for having us,' said Tom. He smiled awkwardly.

'Goodbye, Miss Walker, Bye, Emma,' whispered Stella again.

Emma beamed at her and nodded. 'Safe travels!'

'Well, now. I hope you all had a good day out,' said Miss Cowley. Nancy closed the door behind them just as Mrs Dunford appeared from the back stair.

'We certainly did!' said Lucy. 'Emma's back to normal. We found Jack and went for a picnic. AND

Sophie *bribed a bent copper* to save Jack's adopted brother from the workhouse!'

'Lucy!' said Miss Cowley, taking a step back. 'Did I hear you correctly?'

'*Yep!*' said Lucy, pressing her lips hard together, making a popping sound. She'd been dying to try out this new word and now seemed as good a time as any.

'Goodness me!' said Mrs Dunford. 'I shouldn't let Lady Cuthbertson hear you talk like that!'

'Oh, Mama won't mind!' Lucy's words came thick and fast. 'It was Mr Gladstone who told Sophie about *bent coppers*. They take money to help bad people get out of trouble — except that Sidney hadn't done anything wrong.' Miss Cowley and Mrs Dunford stood back, arms crossed and open-mouthed. 'I bet Mama knows all about them,' Lucy went on. 'What with all her demonstrating, I don't think *coppers* are exactly her best friends! Anyway, I've memorised his number so we can even *report* him if we want to.' She smiled triumphantly and looked around.

'Well, that is certainly all very *eventful!*' said Miss Cowley. 'Lady Cuthbertson will be all ears for the detail when she comes in, I'm sure. Now, would you like to stay for a while, Tom and Stella?'

'I'm afraid we need to get back to our second cousin,' said Stella, glancing at the grandfather clock. 'We're leaving to re-join Mama and Papa tomorrow, so need to spend some time with her. Thank you so much anyway. She's expecting us back through the garden.'

'I do hope your luggage has arrived,' said Lucy quickly. 'I'll come and collect the clothes tomorrow. What time are you leaving?'

'I'm not sure,' said Stella, thankful for Lucy's quick thinking. 'Mama's arranged it — quite early, I think. Here, take your hat at least. And thank you.'

'Nancy will collect the clothes tomorrow, Miss Lucy. No need for you to go,' said Mrs Dunford, looking around. 'She was here a minute ago.'

'Here I am,' she said, coming down the stairs. 'I'd been wondering where this was!' She held up a dusting cloth. 'Must've dropped it when the doorbell rang. Of course, Mrs Dunford. I'll go over to collect the clothes tomorrow.'

Lucy raised her eyebrows and darted a mischievous look at Stella that implied she would *cross that bridge when she came to it*. 'Well,' she said, 'safe travels back.' She stepped forward to hug Tom, and then Stella. *'Take the boat if the moles come,'* she whispered. *'I'll check on you later.'*

'Nancy, will you please see Master Tom and Miss Stella out to the gardens,' said Mrs Dunford.

'Yes, Mrs Dunford.'

. . .

'Here,' said Nancy, putting a paper bag into each of Tom and Stella's hands as she opened the back door for them. 'A little something in case you need it later.'

Stella felt her cheeks flush. 'What is it?' she said, glancing at the clock on the end wall. The time read 5.30 p.m.

'Jus' a bit o' supper to keep you going.' Nancy smiled, then looked over her shoulder and back again. 'Oh, and summat you left upstairs. I don't know what you lot are up to, but I ain't sayin' nothing! I loved sneaking around when I was your age.' She shook her head and rolled her eyes. 'Miss Lucy thinks I don't go in the luggage room, but she's wrong — it's the first place I looked when food went missing. *And* I saw you all hiding in the broom cupboard this morning!' She giggled and looked over her shoulder again. 'You seem like nice children to me. Just tap on the door if you need anything else, but make sure Mrs Dunford's not about. Go on, now, off you go!'

26
LEAVING AND RETURNING

As they headed in the direction of the lake, Stella glanced inside the bag Nancy had handed her. She gasped. 'She's put my phone and notebook in here!' In the panic of the last few hours, she had forgotten about the pouch she'd hidden upstairs. 'How *cool* of her to cover for us like that,' she added, trying to break the ice.

Tom didn't reply. Ever since she'd failed to hand over the note to Jack's mum, he had seemed distant and afraid, angry even. Who could blame him? Finally, with no one around, she could explain. As the lake path came into view, she knew exactly the right place to have their conversation.

Tom marched ahead, leaving her behind as he grasped at his rolled-over trousers under his jacket to keep them from falling down. 'It's okay, Tom,' she called. 'You can be angry with me.' As they made their way down the path to the lake, the hem of her dress snagged on a bush, causing her to stop and unpick the muslin fabric from a thorn. Crouching down, she realised for the second time since they'd arrived just how accustomed she'd become to wearing flowing, lace-topped dresses, something that would have been unthinkable just a few days ago. She jerked her head up. Was this a sign they'd be staying because they couldn't save Jack? She looked towards the lake, picturing home. She missed Mum and Dad, and Hannah — and the future. She stood back up, blinking back welling tears. She had to stay strong for Tom. And she had to prepare him for anything.

As she rounded the corner, Tom was already at the lakeside untying the boat.

'Tom!' she called. 'Shouldn't we wait? What if they don't come tonight?'

'We have to go, Stell!' he called, his voice unwavering. 'If the tunnel disappears—'

She quickly caught up with him on the little jetty. 'Wait a minute, Tom. Think! If the moles don't come, Lucy can't reach us across the lake.' She paused, considering her next words. 'They might not come *for days*.' This was as far as she was prepared to go for now.

'No! We must go over now, Stell! We need to be ready.' Fear and determination shone from his brown eyes. There would be no dissuading him — and she was too weary to fight. They had food for now at least. And if they got stuck on the Island, they'd simply have to row back and find a way to rouse Emma and Lucy, she supposed.

'All right,' she said gently. She reached forward and put the food bag Nancy had given her alongside Tom's in the boat, then helped him steady it as he climbed in. Soon she was alongside him and they were rowing back, one oar each, in the early evening light.

'I'm sorry for not leaving the note with Jack's mum,' she said after a moment's silence. Her voice broke. 'She said we'd find him easily. Then I was pickpocketed in that crowd. By the time I realised—'

'It's fine, Stell.' Tom's voice was calm. For a moment, he seemed older than his years. 'And I would definitely have done the same. We just need to get away, before it's too late.'

She turned to look at him. 'Really? You'd have *really* done the same?'

'*Yes!*' he said, and kept rowing beside her. 'I knew you were worried, and I tried to signal, but with so many people looking it was really hard.'

Stella breathed in slowly, a weight seeming to float away. And now, with her mind much clearer, she suddenly understood why Tom was so desperate to get across the lake. If they made it back to their time where Charlie lived, it meant that Jack somehow *hadn't* travelled on the Titanic after all — or that he'd survived at least. Not everyone perished, after all. The sooner they got up through the tunnel, the sooner he'd be sure Jack was safe. Every minute could count, and he didn't want to risk a second. She tried to ignore the nagging worry that, of course, this all depended on the moles reappearing in the first place, and on the tunnel taking them to the future they knew. As they approached the far bank, her big sister instincts kicked back in. Whether or not the moles danced, and whatever version of their future it took them to if they did appear, she would be there for Tom.

Once on the Island they quickly made their way to the shed to retrieve their clothes and rucksacks. The four days they had been away felt like a lifetime, and Stella's jeans and T-shirt felt tight against her skin as she pulled them on. The temperature had dropped, and she was grateful they'd thought to bring jackets. She held up Lucy's dress in the dying light inside the shed one last time. With her phone battery long dead, taking a picture was out of the question, so she tried to remember each detail so she could draw it for Hannah when they got back. She then rolled the dress into a tube shape, the way she'd seen her mum pack clothes, and placed it in the laundry bag.

Tom was unusually shy and insisted on getting changed in the far corner behind the end of the workbench. Stella blinked in the gloom as she waited, feeling both proud of how much he seemed to have grown up since they were last here, and sad at losing part of the little brother she was so used to looking out for. She still wasn't certain of what lay ahead — and she'd still need to protect him if things didn't work out. But she could see a time soon when they'd be looking out for each other in equal measure.

'Okay, let's bury the bag,' she said after he'd handed her Arthur's clothes. She drew the drawstring tight on the laundry bag and looked up to see Tom already with hoe in hand, and a spade he'd found at the far end of the shed. They quickly located the hole around the back of the shed. The soil was loose, making it quick and easy to dig down. 'There,' said Tom, smoothing over the last of the earth, then roughing it with the corner of the hoe. Stella then gathered some twigs and leaves and scattered them on top.

As they arrived at the foot of the tree, Stella pictured the first time they'd jumped down and seen Jack rowing towards them — his dirt-smudged face and ragged knee-length trousers, and the look of terror in his face as he asked for their help. She bit her lip, thinking of what hung in the balance for him now.

'I'm going to check if the tunnel's there — just in case,' said Tom.

Stella was about to roll her eyes at him but stopped herself. 'You know it won't be,' she said gently. But already he was climbing and was soon high in the branches. Moments later, he dropped to his feet and sat beside her.

'It was worth checking at least,' he said with a sigh as he picked up a twig and began carving lines in the moss beside his feet. The clouds had cleared from earlier, but the last of the sun was hidden behind the trees.

* * *

'I wonder what the time is,' said Stella. 'Lucy's bound to come looking for us at some point.' Several hours had passed. They had long since eaten the food Nancy had given them and there was no sign of the moles.

Ever since the half-moon had appeared through the trees, Tom had been walking up and down as he scanned the far bank. 'They must come soon, Stell,' he said, coming to sit beside her. The earlier confidence in his voice was gone.

'I hope so.' She tried to sound upbeat, despite an

increasingly hollow feeling inside. 'We'll just have to row back if—'

'I can see them! They're over there, Stell!' Tom jumped back up and pointed across the lake to where the path joined the jetty. Stella scrambled to her feet, heart racing, and quickly picked out four moles scuttling in a circle in a shaft of moonlight beside the water. Tom reached to start the climb, just as shadows moving on the far side of the lake farther along caught Stella's eye. She grabbed his arm.

'Look!' she said. Three figures stood waving — the three familiar silhouettes of Lucy, Emma and Sophie in their dark coats and ankle length boots. The moles continued to turn in circles off to one side. Stella put her hand to her mouth, smiling. 'Sophie has seen the moles!' she whispered.

Stella and Tom lifted their arms and waved back, neither daring to call out.

'We'd better go,' said Tom, then turned and led the way.

'Until next time!' whispered Stella. As she looked across the lake one last time, she promised to remember every detail for Hannah.

Stella followed Tom up through the branches. 'The tunnel's here!' he called down, joy in his voice. Stella carried on climbing, the occasional crack of twigs and rustle of leaves cutting through the silence. Moments later, she felt the first rung of the ladder and smelt the familiar damp earth of the tunnel. Feeling her way up without her phone light was easier than she'd imagined, and she soon emerged to join Tom inside the rhododendron bush. Darkness surrounded them as they crawled out into the gardens. As Stella looked to the sky, she breathed out with relief as a faint light reflected in the sky from the streetlamps.

'Stell, I—' Tom started.

'Let's get back,' she replied, suddenly desperate to be in her bedroom. She dashed ahead. The back door was still unlocked, and they slipped quickly in, leaving their shoes on the hallway rack as they passed through.

As Stella opened the door to her room, Tom followed in. 'Stell, you need to see this,' he said, his voice trembling.

'What?' She quickly felt for her bedside lamp and switched it on. Tom stood by her bed, his eyes filled with tears as he began reaching into his little rucksack.

'I had to do it, Stell.' He sat on her bed and pulled out an envelope, folded in two.

'A letter?' said Stella, furrowing her brow as he passed the envelope to her. She shook it, but it felt empty. She lifted the flap and pulled out a flimsy piece of paper. She darted a look at Tom then back at the paper, her mouth now wide open. Centred at the top was a black image of a ship with four funnels, with the words, 'White Star Line' to its right. Below it were the words: 'Ocean Steam Navigation Company Limited of Great Britain. Third Class (Steerage) Passenger Contract Ticket.' A stamp in the middle read 'RMS TITANIC' and the date 10TH APRIL 1912 had been filled in by hand.

'Tom!' she gasped, now looking at the box in the middle where two names had been added in curly handwriting: Jacob Harold Green and Master Jack Charles Green.

'I didn't plan to,' said Tom. 'I saw the envelope above their fireplace.' Stella turned the envelope over and saw the word *Tickets* written in shaky handwriting on the front. 'I've never stolen anything before, Stell. It's why I wanted to get back — before they guessed and came looking for us.'

And now Stella remembered his awkward look and fumbling as he'd emerged from Betty's house, and the strange grimaces that had followed.

'Oh my goodness, Tom!' she whispered, her eyes shining. 'You are *awesome!* You have just saved Jacob and Jack's lives!'

'I didn't save anyone else's, though,' he said, his voice wavering.

Stella put her arms around him. *'You couldn't have,*

Tom. And no one would have believed us if we'd said anything. Like we said.' She let out a deep breath. This was the second time he had saved Jack. How brave and how loyal he was.

She stepped back and gave him a puzzled frown. 'But why didn't you tell me when we left Lucy's?'

A tear escaped and rolled down his cheek. 'They'd have put you in prison if they knew you knew! That's what they *do* with older children there, don't they?' His voice started to crack. 'If we'd got caught—' He sniffed and wiped his face with his sleeve. 'Anyway, that's why I wanted to get back quickly — in case the police came for us. I tried to signal. I'm sorry, Stell.'

'Tom! There's nothing to be sorry for! I'm *so* proud of you!'

She thought for a moment as she held the ticket in front of them. 'What do you think we should do with it?'

They paused, staring at it. A smile finally spread across Tom's face, then they answered in unison. 'Send it to Charlie Green!'

Stella plugged in her phone and set the alarm for 6.30 the next morning — she needed to be sure she was up before her mum.

As she lay back and drifted off, a remark Lucy had

made about the moles appearing just when they were most needed floated through her mind. She was definitely right about that — there was no way they could have saved Emma or Jack without them. But was it *more* than that? She shook her head, trying to arrange confused thoughts. The moles had enabled them to plan to save lives not once, but twice. But what if the moles somehow *were* the plan and their lives were all connected in some deeper, circular way that depended on each other's actions? Her eyelids drooped as she tried to make sense of it all. *'So complicated,'* she whispered, and soon she was asleep.

'Goodness, you look tired,' said Mrs Hawken when she finally came into the kitchen just before eight, carrying a large bag. 'Where's Lucy? Still asleep?'

'I wish!' said Stella with a yawn as she poured milk onto her muesli. 'Her mum collected her at *7 o'clock*, would you believe! Lucy's cat's gone missing — she said they'd been texting each other from six but decided it was too early to wake me up.' She smiled. 'Anyway, I said we had to be *quiet as mice* when I let her out.'

'Well, thank you for that!' said her mum. 'Tom's still dead to the world,' she added with a laugh.

'Probably dreaming of other worlds!' said Stella.

'Talking of other worlds,' said her mum. 'What's

happened to your hair? You look positively Edwardian!

'Oh,' she added. 'Happy Easter!' Then she reached into the bag and plonked two large chocolate eggs on the breakfast table. 'One each. Don't eat them all at once!'

'I don't get it,' said Tom, frowning as they sat on the Island in the gardens later that day. 'How come Mrs Moon never told us she met us again in her time? She said she and Lucy came and found us in the future, when we were much older?'

Stella lay back on the grass and looked at the sky through the branches of the plane trees, then raised her eyebrows. 'Yes, but she didn't say we *wouldn't* meet her before that, did she?'

'Maybe she didn't *want* us to know!' said Tom. 'You know — in case it messed things up. That's what she said about not telling us about Harry going missing when we asked, remember?'

Stella narrowed her eyes as the sun popped out from behind a cloud. 'You know what that means, don't you?' she said, twisting her head to look at him with a smile. 'Maybe there are *other* adventures she didn't tell us about...'

She lay back down, smiling.

'Maybe...'

EPILOGUE

On the afternoon of 12th April 1912, three days before the sinking of RMS Titanic on her maiden voyage, a gentleman out strolling on Tooting Bec Common picked up a small, muddied envelope with the letter 'J' on the front. Someone had ripped it open. A note sat inside.

He tutted and shook his head. Either the thief had taken any money and discarded the rest — or had been disappointed at finding no money. He pulled the note out and read the message.

Don't go on Titanic! <u>Urgent.</u>
Repeat.
<u>DON'T GO ON BOAT!</u>
TS

He frowned. Then arched his eyebrows. Then he glanced around. Finding no litter bin, he pushed the note deep into his coat pocket and went on his way. By the time he got home, distracted by the signs of a head cold, he'd forgotten all about it.

Four days later, the sinking of the Titanic filled newspaper headlines around the world. By this time, the same gentleman was bedridden with a fever.

Two weeks later, the gentleman's wife, while checking his pockets for his gloves, found the note. When she handed it to her husband, who was up and about for the first time in 14 days, he arched his eyebrows once more.

The following day, he paid a visit to the offices of *The Times* newspaper where his good friend Alfred Bates was a subeditor in need of a break. The day after that, a small piece ran on the inside front page, headlined as follows:

DID TOOTING BEC NOTE PREDICT SINKING OF TITANIC?

It was a short piece, and one of many conspiracy theories that always surfaced after major disasters. Nevertheless, Henry Gladstone and his neighbour Lord Cuthbertson both made a point of reading *The Times* each day, and the conspiracy headline caught the eye of each.

.   .   .

'My goodness — that's exactly where Lucy was the other week!' said Lady Cuthbertson as her husband passed her the paper.

'Weren't the girls at Tooting Bec around that time, Constance?' said Henry Gladstone to his wife. He paused and shook his head. 'Damned lucky Jacob and Jack's tickets were stolen,' he added. 'I've said it once, and I'll say it again. We owe the culprit a favour — and I'm delighted to hear they've abandoned all plans to leave our shores. Jacob really is one of a kind.'

At this point, he had peered down the breakfast table. 'Did I tell you Jacob said Jack was having second thoughts anyway, after that dreadful business with his adopted brother? Apparently, he wants to be a gardener when he finishes school.'

'Does he now?' said Constance Gladstone, looking out to the communal gardens with a smile. 'Well, I'm sure you can pull some strings on that front when the time comes, dear.'

'Indeed,' said Henry Gladstone, reaching for his coffee cup. 'Now, where was I before being distracted by conspiracy theories…?'

.   .   .

So it was that Emma, Sophie and Lucy learned belatedly of the lost note intended for Jack. They were able to tell him about it not long afterwards, after imploring Henry Gladstone to take them to see him. It was at that same visit Jack told them of the tickets going missing the day they were last there, and that he was sure he had Tom to thank for saving his and Jacob's lives.

PLEASE WRITE A REVIEW!

If you enjoyed *RETURN TO THE SECRET LAKE*, please leave a short review on Amazon or your other preferred bookstore's website. It will help other families find this page-turning time travel adventure! Please ask an adult to help you.

You can also leave a review at ***thesecretlake.com*** where Karen will always reply.

TOP TIP: DON'T GIVE AWAY ANY SECRETS IN YOUR REVIEW!

The Secret Lake — the adventure continues

To be the first to know when *The Secret Lake 3* will be out, visit **kareninglisauthor.com** and sign up to Karen's Readers' Club.

MORE DETAILS OVERLEAF >>

JOIN KAREN'S READERS' CLUB
FREE POSTERS, SNEAK PREVIEWS & MORE!

Join Karen's Readers' Club newsletter and get:

- Free artwork and posters from Karen's books
- 'Sneak peek' previews of works in progress (story excerpts, illustrations, book covers)
- The chance to request advance reader copies of Karen's upcoming books
- The chance to give feedback on character names, book covers, titles, story ideas
- Advance notice of special offers, book launches (including *The Secret Lake 3*), and online and in-person author events

Find out more at
kareninglisauthor.com/readers-club

ABOUT THE AUTHOR

Karen Inglis is an international bestselling children's author who lives in London, England. She writes picture books for ages 3-6, chapter books for ages 6-8, and middle-grade novels for ages 8-12. Her middle-grade time travel adventure *The Secret Lake* has sold over 400,000 copies in the English language and is in translation around the world.

Parents/teachers: sign up to Karen's children's books occasional newsletter at **kareninglisauthor.com** for news about **book releases, virtual and live events, special offers** and **teaching resources.** You can also follow Karen online below.

facebook.com/kareninglisauthor

twitter.com/kareninglis

instagram.com/kareninglis_childrensbooks

ALSO BY KAREN INGLIS

ORDER ONLINE OR FROM LOCAL BOOKSHOPS

The Secret Lake (8-11 yrs)

A lost dog, a hidden time tunnel and a secret lake take Stella and Tom to their home and the children living there 100 years in the past. Almost half a million copies sold and in translation around the world.

Eeek! The Runaway Alien (7-10 yrs)

Soccer-mad Charlie can't believe his luck when he opens his door to an alien one morning — a football-loving alien who has come to Earth for the World Cup! *'Laugh-out-loud funny!'* ~ LoveReading4KidsUK.

Walter Brown and the Magician's Hat (7-10 yrs)

A boy, a magic top hat and a talking cat spell magical mayhem after Walter inherits his Great Grandpa Horace's magician's hat on his 10th birthday. *Red Ribbon Winner ~ Wishing Shelf Book Awards UK.*

Henry Haynes and the Great Escape (6-8 yrs)

A boy, a magic library book and a bossy boa — oh, and a VERY smelly gorilla with a zoo escape plan! Fun and fast-paced for early readers. Black and white illustrations.

The Tell-Me Tree (4-8 yrs)

'Hello, I am the Tell-Me Tree. Why don't you come and sit by me? Tell me your worries. Tell me your cares. Share your best dreams, or your scary nightmares.'

Praised by parents, teachers and children's charities, and being used extensively in UK classrooms. Comes with free printable download activities.

The Christmas Tree Wish (3-6 yrs)

A heartwarming tale about hope, friendship and being different. *Shortlisted for the UK Selfies Award, 2020.*

Ferdinand Fox's Big Sleep (3-5 yrs)

'Ferdinand Fox curled up in the sun, as the church of St Mary struck quarter past one…'

This colour picture book delights with its rhyming text and vibrant illustrations.

Ferdinand Fox and the Hedgehog (3-6 yrs)

'Ferdinand Fox trotted down past the park, where the seesaws and swings stood still in the dark…That very same night, seeking bugs with her snout, Hatty the hedgehog was out and about…'

Introducing Hatty the hedgehog and her baby son Ed. Eight pages of fun facts about foxes and hedgehogs. Perfect for little ones. Also comes with free colouring sheets to download.